TO THEM THE MUSIC OF THE STARS WAS A *DANSE MACABRE!*

They stared at the body. The man was dead—every symptom indicated this. Yet the body moved, quivered, twitched—and gave a hint of the secret horror that awaited man in the outer reaches of space.

All signs pointed to the fact that no human could come back alive from Barnard's Star. Something elusive, beyond comprehension, existed out there; something that was a perpetual bait, a perpetual trap. But Comyn knew he had to join that second fated mission. For somewhere beyond the veil of the Transuranae lay the answer to the question that was more important than life to him.

A novel of great imaginative force by the author of THE SWORD OF RHIANNON and THE COMING OF THE TERRANS.

CAST OF CHARACTERS

COMYN

He followed a will o' the wisp to the very brink of his own extinction.

BALLANTYNE

His quivering hand drew a path to an unknown star.

WILLIAM STANLEY

The key he held might possibly open the treasure-house of the universe.

PETER COCHRANE

He powered a starship with his own personal drive for profit.

VICKREY

Though born on Earth, he had become a native of an unearthly planet.

PAUL ROGERS

He was both the object of an interplanetary search and the means of an interstellar discovery.

THE BIG JUMP

by

LEIGH BRACKETT

ACE BOOKS, INC.
1120 Avenue of the Americas
New York, N.Y. 10036

I

Across the gulfs between the worlds, from end
to end of a Solar System poised taut and trembling on the
verge of history, the rumors flew. Somebody's made it, the
Big Jump. Somebody came back.

Spacemen talking, in the bars around a thousand ports.
People talking, in the streets of countless cities. *Somebody's
done it—the Big Jump—done it and come back. That last
bunch, they—Ballantyne's outfit. They say . . .*

They said a lot of things, conflicting, fantastic, impossible, grim. But behind the words there was only rumor, and
behind the rumors—silence. A silence that was sphinx-like
as the soundless wastes of night that roll forever around the
island Sun. Too much silence. That was what Arch Comyn
listened to, after he had heard the words. The rumors themselves seemed to have come most strongly along a line that
ran from Pluto's orbit in to Mars, and it was around Mars
that the silence was deepest.

Comyn went to Mars.

The guard at the main gate said, "Sorry. You got to have
a pass."

"Since when?" asked Comyn.

"Since a couple of weeks."

"Yeah? What's so different about the Cochrane Company all of a sudden, now?"

"It ain't only us, it's every spaceship line on Mars. Too many creeps wanting answers to silly questions. You got business here, you get a pass through the regular channels. Otherwise blow."

Comyn glanced briefly at the height and size of the locked main gate, and then at the steel-and-glassite box that housed the guard and the controls.

"Okay," he said. "You don't need to get tough about it."

He turned and walked away to where his rented car was waiting, and got in. He drove slowly back along the strip of concrete road that led to the new, prosaic, and completely earthly city four miles away. Out here on the open desert the cold Martian wind blew thin and dry and edged with dust, and there was no comfort in the far red line of the horizon, naked under a dark blue sky.

Presently there was another road veering off from the one he was on, and he turned into it. It went round to the truck gate of the spaceport, which showed now as a low sprawling monster on his left, with clusters of buildings and a couple of miles of sheds grouped around the docking area. The nine-globed insigne of the Cochranes showed even at this distance on the tall control tower.

Halfway between the main road and the truck gate, and out of sight of both, Comyn slewed his car into the ditch. He climbed out, leaving the door open, and sat down in the dust. Nothing used this road but company equipment. All he had to do was wait.

The wind blew, laggard, wandering, sad, like an old man searching in the wilderness for the cities of his youth, the bright cities that had been and now were not. The red dust formed tiny riffles around Comyn's feet. He sat, not stirring, waiting with a timeless patience, thinking . . .

Two days and nights I spent in the lousy bars here, with my ears spread to the breeze. And it was all for the birds, except for that one drunken kid. If he wasn't telling the truth . . .

There was a sound on the road. A truck coming out from

the city, bearing the Cochrane name. Comyn lay down quietly in the dust.

The truck roared up, raced past, screeched to a stop, and then backed up. The driver got out. He was a young man, big and burly, burned dark by the Martian wind. He leaned over the body beside the road.

Comyn came up off the ground and hit him.

The trucker didn't want to stay down. He was mad, and Comyn didn't blame him for it. It took another hard blow to put him out. Comyn dragged him around behind the car and searched his pockets. He had a pass, all right. Comyn took his coverall and the cap with the broad peak and green visor that cut down desert glare. Then he fixed the trucker up inside the car so he'd keep safe until he got loose or somebody found him. On an impulse, Comyn dug out a couple of crumpled bills, hesitated, then shoved one of them into the trucker's pocket.

"Buy yourself a drink," he said to the unhearing ears. "On me."

Dressed in the company coverall, wearing the company cap with the face-shielding visor, and driving the company truck, Comyn rolled up to the gate and showed his pass. The guard opened up and waved him in.

One of the great sleek Cochrane ships was on the field, loading passengers for somewhere. Around the docks and the sheds and the machine shops there was a clangorous turmoil where the work of servicing and refueling went on, with the huge mobile cargo cranes stalking mightily through the confusion. Comyn glanced at it without interest, got his bearings, and turned the truck toward the administration area.

Warehouses. Office blocks. Enough buildings for a small city. Comyn drove slowly, squinting at signs, not seeing the one he wanted. The palms of his hands sweated on the wheel and he wiped them one after the other on his coverall. His belly was tied up in knots inside.

That kid had better be right, he thought. *I better be right. I'm in trouble all the way now, and it better be for something.*

He leaned out of the cab and hailed a passing clerk. "Which way to the hospital? I'm new around here."

7

The clerk gave him directions and he drove on, around two or three corners and down a narrow street. He found the hospital, a shiny white building designed for the care of Cochrane employees, not very big and tucked away in a quiet place. There was an alley behind it and a door that said Delivery Entrance.

Comyn pulled the truck in, cut the motor, and got out. The door was only a step or two away, but before he could reach it the door had opened and closed again, and there was a man standing in front of it.

Comyn smiled. The knots in his middle went away. "Hello," he said cheerfully, and added in his mind, *I love you, little man with the hard look and the gun under your jacket. Seeing you means I'm right.*

"What you got there, buddy?" asked the man in the doorway.

What Comyn had was a load of baggage destined for some ship. But he said, "Stuff for the hospital commissary. Perishable." He let the words drift him a little closer. "I've got the bills." He put his hand in his pocket, still smiling, a man without a care in the world.

With the beginning of suspicion, the man in the doorway said, "How come you're so early? The usual time for delivery—"

"What I've got," said Comyn softly, "can be delivered any time. No, keep your hands right where they are. I've got something here in my pocket, and if it goes off you'll know what it is. But you won't like it."

The man stood taut against the door, frozen in mid-motion, his eyes focused on Comyn's right hand that was hidden in his pocket. He was thinking hard, thinking of all the small, nasty, illegal weapons that ingenious people on nine different worlds had created and successfully used. He was not pleased with his thoughts.

Comyn said, "Let's go inside."

The man hesitated. His eyes met Comyn's, searched them, probed them. Then he made a small snarling sound and turned to open the door.

"Quietly," said Comyn. "And if there's anyone around, you vouch for me."

There was no one in this back corridor lined with store-rooms. Comyn shoved the guard into the nearest one and kicked the door shut. "I'll take that gun," he said, and took it. A nice neat shocker, the latest model. Comyn shifted it to his right hand and stepped back.

"That's better," he said. "For a minute I thought you were going to call me out there."

The man's face became vicious. "You mean you didn't have—"

"I have now." Comyn's thumb flicked the stud up to lethal voltage. "Save your mad till later. Where's Ballantyne?"

"Ballantyne?"

"Who is it, then? Strang? Kessel? Vickrey?" He paused. "Paul Rogers?" His voice hardened. "Who have the Cochranes got in here?"

"I don't know."

"What do you mean, you don't know? You're guarding somebody. You have to know who it is."

Beads of sweat had begun to glisten on the man's face. He was watching Comyn, and he had forgotten to be angry.

"Look. They brought somebody in here, sure. They're keeping him under guard, sure. It's supposed to be one of our own guys, with something contagious. Maybe I believe that, maybe I don't. But all I know is that I sit on that back door eight hours a day. The Cochranes don't tell me their business. They don't tell anybody."

"Yeah," said Comyn. "You know where the room is."

"It's guarded too."

"That's where you come in." He spoke briefly and the man listened, staring unhappily at his own weapon in Comyn's hard sunburned fist.

"I guess," he said, "I've got to do it."

He did it. He took Comyn without a hitch through the main corridors and upstairs into a small wing of private rooms that were all vacant except for one at the end. In front of that one sat a large man, half asleep.

That's what the kid in the bar had been mad about. They had thrown him out of one of these rooms and put him into a ward. He had been the only patient in the wing—and why had they thrown him out, suddenly, in the middle of the night?

The large man came out of his doze and sprang up.

"It's all right, Joe," said the man who walked so close to Comyn. "This guy's a friend of mine."

His voice carried no note of conviction. The large man started forward. "Are you crazy, bringing a stranger— Hey . . . hey, what goes on?"

His reflexes were good, very good. But Comyn was already set and in range. The shocker made a gentle buzzing sound and the large man hit the floor. The smaller one followed him, a short second behind. Both men were out, but nothing worse. Comyn had had the shocker back on low power long before he used it.

When the young doctor looked out of the end room a moment later, disturbed by the faint sounds that had reached him, there was nothing to see but the empty hall with the empty rooms along it.

He said, "Joe?" on a tentative note, but there was no answer. Frowning, he went down to the intersecting corridor to have a look. While his back was turned Comyn slipped into the end room and shut the door. There was a lock on it, brand new and shiny, non-regulation equipment for a hospital room. He snapped it and then he turned toward the bed, toward the man who lay there. His heart was hammering now because after all it might be somebody else . . .

And the rumors were all true. Ballantyne had done it. He had made the Big Jump and come back, back from the outer darkness beyond the sun. The first of all men, come back from the stars.

Comyn bent over the bed. His hands were gentle now, uncertain, touching the skeletal shoulder with a kind of awe.

"Ballantyne," he whispered. "Ballantyne, wake up. Where is Paul?"

He felt bones under his fingers, skin and bones and a tracery of fragile veins. There was movement, a faint pulsation of it, a twitching and quivering of the flesh that never

stopped, as though some dreadful memory still drove the
ravaged body toward escape. A face . . .

It was a face that was only a ghostly echo, pitiful, terrible,
marked by something frightening, worse than death or the
fear of dying. It was something, Comyn thought, that had
never before oppressed the children of Sol. A queer terror
came over him as he looked at it. Suddenly he wanted to
run, to get away out of the room, far away from whatever
evil shadow it was that this man had brought back with
him from another star.

But he stayed. The doctor came and tried the door, bat-
tered on it, yelled, and finally ran away. And still Comyn
bent over the bed and whispered, growing colder, growing
sicker, flinching from the touch of damp skin twitching under
his fingers. And still the terrible face rebuked him and
would not speak.

More men came and shouted outside the door. This time
they brought an electric drill to cut away the lock.

"Ballantyne! What happened to Paul? *Paul* . . . do you
hear? Where is he?"

The drill began to bite on the plastic door.

"Paul," said Comyn patiently. "Where is Paul Rogers?"

The harsh whining of the drill crept around the little
room, filling the corners, filling the silence. Ballantyne moved
his head.

Comyn bent over, so that his ear was almost touching the
blue transparent lips. A voice came out of them, no louder
than the beating of a moth's wing . . .

". . . listened too long. Too long, too far . . ."

"Where is Paul?"

". . . too far, too lonely. We weren't meant for this.
Desolation . . . darkness . . . stars . . ."

Again, almost fiercely, "Where is Paul?"

"Paul . . ."

The drill hit metal. The whining changed to a thin-edged
screech.

The breathing skeleton that was Ballantyne went rigid.
Its lips moved under Comyn's ear, laboring with a dreadful
urgency.

"Don't listen, Paul! I can't go back alone, I can't! Don't

11

listen to them calling . . . Oh, God, why did it have to be transuranic, why did it?"

The drill screeched thinner, higher. And the painful whisper rose.

"The Transuranae! Paul, no! Paul, Paul, Paul . . ."

Suddenly Ballantyne screamed.

Comyn sprang back from the bed, blundering into the wall and staying there, pressed against it, bathed in an icy sweat. Ballantyne screamed, not saying anything, not opening his eyes, just screaming, out of an abysmal agony of soul.

Comyn stretched out his hand to the door and tore it open. The drill-shaft snapped. Men poured into the room and he told them, "For God's sake, make him stop!"

And then, between two heartbeats, Ballantyne was dead.

II

TIME HAD lost itself somewhere in the haze. He was not even sure where he was any more. There was a taste in his mouth, a red and salty taste that he remembered from getting hit in fights. Only there didn't seem to be any fight going on. And when he tried to see, all he could get was a blurred confusion of light and shadow in which things vaguely moved.

The questions still came. They were part of the universe, part of existence. He could not remember a time when there had not been questions. He hated them. He was tired and his jaws hurt, and it was hard to answer. But he had to, because when he didn't somebody hit him again, somebody he couldn't quite manage to get at and kill, and he didn't like that.

"Who paid you to do this, Comyn? Who sent you after Ballantyne?"

"Nobody."

"What's your job?"

"Construction boss." The words came out thick and slow and painful. They had worn grooves in his tongue from being said so often.

"Who are you working for?"

Double question. Tricky. But the answer was the same. "Nobody."

"Who did you work for?"

"Inter-World Engineering . . . bridges . . . dams . . . spaceports. I quit."

"Why?"

"To find Ballantyne."

"Who told you it was Ballantyne?"

"Nobody. Rumor. Could have been any of 'em. Could have been . . . Paul."

"Who's Paul?"

"Paul Rogers. Friend."

"He was the flight engineer on Ballantyne's ship, wasn't he?"

"No. Astrophys—" He couldn't handle that one. "Something to do with stars."

"How much did United Tradelines pay you to get to Ballantyne?"

"Nothing. On my own."

"And you found out Paul Rogers is dead."

"No."

"Ballantyne told you he was alive?"

"No."

This was the hard part. This was the worst of it. At first reason had told him: keep your jaw shut. As long as they aren't sure, you'll have a chance: they won't kill you. Now it was only deaf, blind instinct. Comyn weaved his head from side to side, trying to get up, to get away. But he couldn't, he was tied.

"What did Ballantyne tell you, Comyn?"

"Nothing."

The flat palm gently jarred his brain.

"You were locked up with him for nearly twenty minutes. We heard his voice. What did he say, Comyn?"

"He screamed. That's all."

The cupped palm, bursting his eardrum, cracked his skull down the middle.

"What did he tell you, Comyn?"

"Nothing!"

The gentle approach. "Listen, Comyn, we're all tired. Let's quit fooling around. Just tell us what Ballantyne said and we can all go home and sleep. You'd like that, Comyn —a nice soft bed and nobody to bother you. Just tell us."

"Didn't talk. Just . . . screamed."

The other approach. "Okay, Comyn. You're a big guy. You got scars on your knuckles. You think you're tough, and you are—oh, yes, a very big muscular iron-headed character. But they don't come so tough they can't be softened."

Fists this time, or whatever they were using. The slow dribble of blood down the side of his face, into his mouth, into his eyes. Pain in his belly.

"What did Ballantyne say?"

"Nothing . . ." A faint whisper, trailing off.

Voices, jumbled, distant. *Let him rest, he's nearly out. . . . Rest, hell, give me the ammonia.* The biting fumes, the gasp, the partial return of light. And it began again. *Who told you we had Ballantyne? Who are you working for? What did Ballantyne say?*

There came a time when Comyn thought he heard the opening of a door and then a new voice, angry, authoritative. He sensed a sudden change going on, things or people moving quickly in the reddish half-blind obscurity. Somebody was doing something with his hands. Instinct told him when they were free. He rose and struck out, hit something that yelled, caught it and held on with a single-hearted desire to tear it in pieces. Then it slipped away, everything slipped away, and there was only darkness and a great peace. . . .

He woke up gradually, as out of a long sleep. He was in a very comfortable bedroom, and a stranger was standing over him with a certain air of impatience. He was a youngish, well-fed, sandy-haired man who looked as though he carried the weight of the world on his shoulders and considered Comyn an unwelcome addition to the burden, one he wanted to be done with as soon as possible.

Comyn let him stand, until he had dredged up what memories he possessed and got them in order. Then he sat up, very slowly and carefully, and the stranger spoke.

"No internal injuries and no broken bones, Mr. Comyn. We've done all we could for the bruises. You've been here two days."

Comyn grunted. He felt his face, touching it lightly.

"Our doctors did their best there, too. They assure me there won't be a scar."

"That's fine. Thanks very much," Comyn said sourly, and looked up. "Who are you?"

"My name is Stanley, William Stanley. I'm business manager for the Cochrane enterprises here on Mars. Look here, Mr. Comyn." Stanley bent over him, frowning. "I want you to understand that this was done to you absolutely without

15

the knowledge or sanction of the management. I was away on business, or it would never have happened."

"I'll bet," said Comyn. "Since when have the Cochranes objected to a little blood?"

Stanley sighed. "The old reputation is hard to live down, even though it was made two generations ago. We employ a lot of men, Mr. Comyn. Sometimes some of them make mistakes. This was one of them. The Cochranes apologize." He paused, and then added, making sure that Comyn got every word quite clearly, "We felt that the best apology lay in not pressing charges against you for some rather serious offenses."

"I guess that makes us even," Comyn said.

"Good. Your papers, passport, and wallet are on the table there beside you. In those boxes on the chair you'll find clothing to replace your own, which was beyond repair. Passage home to Earth has been arranged for you on the next Cochrane liner. And I think that's all."

"Not quite," said Comyn, and got stiffly out of bed. The room went round him twice, and then steadied. He looked at Stanley from under sullen brows and laughed.

"Next step in the game, huh? You couldn't beat anything out of me, so now you'll try sweetness and light. Who are you trying to kid?"

Stanley's mouth tightened. "I don't understand you."

Comyn's gesture was sweepingly contemptuous. "You're not going to let me run loose with what I know."

"Exactly what do you know, Mr. Comyn?" asked Stanley with a curious politeness.

"Ballantyne. You had him here, hidden, in secret, when the whole System was waiting to welcome him back. You, the Cochranes, trying to grab away from him whatever he'd found! Dirty pool and dirty hands playing it. Where's his ship? Where are the men who went with him? Where have you got *them* hidden?"

Anger was in Comyn's voice, a dark flush of anger in his cheeks. His hands moved in short, hungry circles.

"Ballantyne made the Big Jump, he and the men with him. They did the biggest thing men have ever done. They reached out and touched the stars. And you tried to hide it, to cover up, to rob them even of the glory they had coming! So now you're going to turn me loose to tell the System what you've done? The hell you are."

Stanley looked at him for a long moment: a big furious man standing naked and incongruous in the handsome bedroom, the half-healed marks and bruises on him, still looking for something to hit. When he spoke it was almost with pity.

"I'm sorry to take the wind out of your sails so cruelly, but I broke the news two days ago, as soon as Ballantyne was dead. Far from trying to rob him, we were making every effort to save his life—without benefit of sensation-hungry mobs, invading newsmen, and people like you. Everybody seems to feel quite grateful toward us."

Comyn sat down slowly on the bed. He said something, but the words were not audible.

"As to the other men . . ." Stanley shook his head. "Ballantyne was alone in the ship. The controls were almost completely automatic, and it was possible for one man to operate them. He was . . . as you saw him. He never knew he had made it back."

"A hell of a thing," said Comyn quietly. "A real hell of a thing. What about the ship itself—and the log? Ballantyne's log. What did it say about Paul Rogers?"

"That's all public knowledge. You can read it in any paper."

"I want to know. What happened to Paul Rogers?"

Stanley studied him curiously. "He must have meant a lot to you to make you go to such lengths."

"He saved my neck once," said Comyn briefly. "We were friends."

Stanley shrugged. "I can't help you. The log and the various scientific data gathered on the outward trip were all clear up to the time they approached the worlds of Barnard's Star. After that—nothing."

"Nothing at all?" Comyn's blood began to stir with a deep and almost unpleasant excitement. If that was true, the score or so of words he had heard from Ballantyne's lips were worth—what? Kingships, empires—a damn sight more, for sure, than the life of one Arch Comyn.

Stanley answered, "No. There's no hint of what happened afterward. The log simply broke off."

Comyn's eyes, very cold and catlike, examined Stanley's face minutely. "I think you're lying."

Stanley began to get an ugly look around the mouth. "Look here, Comyn, all things considered I think you've been treated pretty decently. And if I were you I'd go away quietly without trying everybody's patience too far."

"Yes," said Comyn reflectively. "I guess so." He went over to the boxes on the chair and began to open them. "It would strain your patience pretty hard, wouldn't it, if I asked about the Ballantyne drive? The star-drive he developed, the first and only one that worked. Did you happen to take a look at it?"

"We did. And we did more." Suddenly Stanley was facing him across the chair, his words coming sharp, and rapid, every line of him altered by a startling intensity. "You annoy me, Comyn. You make me sick, battering your way in where you haven't any business and making trouble for everybody. So I'll explain to you, speaking as a Cochrane, because I married into the family and consider myself part of it, and I'm tired of all the two-bit ciphers in the System taking cracks at it.

"We saved Ballantyne's ship from smashing head-on into Pluto. We'd had patrols out looking for it for weeks, of course, and we beat some others to it. We took the ship to our emergency field on Cochrane Beta in the asteroid belt, and we dismantled the Ballantyne drive. Then we flew it to the Cochrane estate on Luna, where nobody else can get at it. And I'll tell you why.

"Every one of these attempts to make the Big Jump has been backed by us or another corporation, or a government that could put up the capital. No private individual could do it. Ballantyne developed that drive with Cochrane money. He built his ship with it, made his flight with it. It's bought and paid for. Now are there any more questions you want to ask?"

"No," said Comyn slowly. "No, I think that's enough for one day."

He began pulling the clothes out of the box. Stanley

swung around and started for the door. His eyes still glittered. Just before he reached it Comyn said:

"You think I'm lying, too."

Stanley shrugged. "I expect you'd have talked if you'd had anything to say. And I doubt very much that you could have brought Ballantyne back to consciousness when all the doctors had failed."

He went out, smacking the door shut hard behind him. *And there it is,* thought Comyn bleakly. *A door slammed right in my face. The Cochranes are all fine, law-abiding people; Ballantyne's dead; the log book has nothing in it— and where do I go from here?*

Home, probably. Home to Earth, with Ballantyne's ghostly voice whispering *transuranic* in his ears, with Ballantyne's awful screaming ringing in his soul. What had they found out there, those five who had reached the stars? What can a man see under this sun or another to put the look on his face that Ballantyne had had?

He thought about those few disjointed words and what they might mean. Ballantyne had landed, somewhere on the worlds of Barnard's Star. And he had left Paul Rogers there, with Strang and Kessel and Vickrey and something called the Transuranae.

Comyn shuddered. There was a tingling on his skin and a taste of something evil in his mouth. All of a sudden he was sorry he had ever come to seek out Ballantyne and got himself entangled in the trailing edges of a shadow cast by an alien sun. If only Ballantyne hadn't screamed . . .

And now the Cochranes were going to let him run a while. They didn't really believe that Ballantyne had remained quiet. They couldn't afford to risk believing it. There were too many others as hungry as they were for the stars, and Comyn—if he liked—could make himself rich by offering what he knew to the highest bidder. A corollary thought evolved itself, and Comyn turned it over in his mind. It seemed to make sense. The Cochranes, on the other hand, didn't know what Comyn knew, and they would let him live as long as possible on the chance that they could get it out of him. That was the reason for the beating and the reason for this so-called freedom he now had.

It dawned on Comyn that he was in trouble, way in, over his head. He had expected trouble with the Cochranes. He had, in fact, come looking for it. But things had got fouled up, and here he was in the middle of something so big he couldn't even guess the end of it. It was a game for stars, and he, Arch Comyn, held just one little hole card . . .

But, whatever the Cochranes did to him, he was going to find out about Paul Rogers.

III

EARTH was one long howling shriek of excitement. Comyn had been back in New York for four days, and the frenzy had shown no signs of calming down. If anything, it was worse.

Nobody slept. Nobody seemed to work. Nobody even went home any more. They lived in the bars, in the streets, in the video houses. They swarmed around the public communications outlets and swirled in thick purposeless torrents up and down the canyon streets. It was like New Year's Eve a thousand times enlarged.

The Big Jump had been made. Man had finally reached the stars, and every clerk and shopgirl, every housewife, businessman and bum felt a personal hysteria of pride and achievement. They swayed in dense masses across Times Square feeling big with a sense of history, sensing the opening drumbeats of an epoch in what they saw and heard from the huge news-service screens.

They talked. They drank and wept and laughed, and a surprising number of them, thinking of the vastness of galactic space and the many stars that there were in it, went into the churches and prayed. Suddenly it seemed as though some very doubtful doors had been opened upon them.

Comyn had spent most of the four days since he landed prowling the streets. Like everybody else, he was too restless to stay in his room. But he had a different reason. He let the crowds drift him where they would, shouldering his way at intervals into one bar or another, drinking steadily but not too much—and thinking.

He had a lot to think about: life and death, the few last words of a man, the Cochranes, and a game of chess that was being played with stars for pawns.

Stars, thought Comyn, *and me. There I am, right up in front and all ready to get knocked over, unless I can figure the right way to jump.*

It took some figuring. And the problem was made tougher by the fact that he was no longer alone, even when he brushed his teeth. Out of doors, wherever he went, a shadow went with him. Indoors, in his furnished room, the privacy was only a hollow sham. Listening and scanning devices had been installed almost as soon as he rented a place. He knew it, but hadn't bothered to try to find them all and tear them out. The longer he kept the Cochranes guessing, the better.

They're waiting, he thought. *Waiting for me to make my play.*

And what was his play going to be? The Cochranes, who had made nine planets their back yard, were in this for wealth and power as wide as the stars. He had horned in for only one thing: to find out what had become of Paul Rogers.

It hadn't been a very bright thing to do. But then Rogers hadn't been very bright either, to stick his own irreproachable neck out for a not-so-irreproachable mugg named Comyn who had got himself into very bad trouble. And Rogers had done that for no better reason than that they had lived on the same street and stolen apples together a long time ago.

But bright or not, it was done, and he couldn't get out of it. The only thing left was to buck the Cochranes.

He had studied the published reports of the finding of Ballantyne's ship and what was in it. Every account agreed that Ballantyne's logbooks broke off short with the approach to the system of Barnard's Star. That meant either that the Cochranes were lying and had secreted one or more of the most vital books for their own uses, or that the Cochranes were not lying and knew no more than anyone else whether Ballantyne had landed or what he had found.

If that was true, he, Comyn, was the only man alive who did know. He might, just possibly, have a weapon big enough, with which to tackle the Cochranes. Or he might, just as possibly, have nothing but his own death warrant.

In either case, it seemed a good idea to find out a little more about the meaning of a certain word. And that, at least, would be easy. Inter-World Engineering had research labs in the same building that housed their home offices. Nobody could get suspicious if he went to the main office under cover of trying to get his job back.

He went there, and the now-familiar unobtrusive form in the nondescript clothes went with him, as far as it could. Comyn left it outside the building. But while he was waiting for the lift, a combination of polished marble, light, and reflection from the doors revealed to him a thing that sent a quick cold chill streaking up his back.

He had not one shadow, but two.

He rode up to Inter-World's floor filled with an unpleasant sense of wonder. The Cochranes on his tail he could understand. But who else? And—why?

From the main office he went up a flight of private stairs to the labs and asked for Dubman, a physicist he had got to know briefly during a sloppy Venusian spaceport project.

Dubman was a brilliant little man who had turned waspish on the world because his liver wouldn't let him drink any more. He stared when Comyn asked him,

"Can you tell me something about transuranic elements?"

"I'm not busy enough, I've got to teach high-school physics to workbosses," Dubman siad. "Look, there's a library with textbooks of physics in it. Good-bye."

"I only want a fast breakdown," Comyn protested. "And it's important."

"Don't tell me work-gang slavedrivers have to know nuclear physics now!"

Comyn decided to tell the truth—at least, part of it. "It isn't that. There's somebody I've got to impress, and I've got to know enough about this to make a stall."

Dubman jeered. "Are you going in for intellectual girls now? That's new. I remember hearing about your exploits and I never—"

Patiently, Comyn steered him back to the subject.

Dubman said, "Transuranic elements are elements that by our natural laws shouldn't be—and aren't."

He paused, proud of his epigram.

Comyn said, "Yeah. Meaning?"

"Meaning," said Dubman, irritated by the lack of appreciation, "that there are ninety-two chemical elements that make up everything in our solar system. They run from hydrogen, number one, the lightest, to uranium, number ninety-two, the heaviest, and most complex."

"I got that far in school," Comyn told him.

"Did you? I wouldn't have guessed it, Comyn. Well, back in 1945 they added something. They built up artificial elements heavier than uranium, neptunium, number ninety-three, and plutonium, number ninety-four. Transuranic elements, that didn't exist naturally on Earth or our other planets at all, but could be made to exist artificially. That was only the start. They kept building more and more complex transuranic elements, and finally Petersen proved . . ."

He was off into technicalities, until Comyn pulled him out of them rudely.

"Listen, that's enough to go on. What I want to know most is: would transuranic elements have any financial importance, and how?"

Dubman looked at him more closely. "So this isn't a wench, after all? What kind of a game are you up to, Comyn?"

"I told you. I just want to run a bluff on someone."

"Well, anyone with two-bits' worth of education will call your bluff. But in answer to your question: we get our atomic power from the heaviest elements, uranium, radium, thorium, and so on. Transuranic elements are heavier. Some of them can't be handled. Others are packed with power but prohibitively expensive and obtainable only in small quantities. Does that answer you?"

"Yeah," said Comyn. "That's answer enough." He walked out, brooding.

Answer enough. Even with his limited knowledge of science, it was brilliantly obvious to him what the discovery of natural transuranic elements, in probably as plentiful supply as the high-number elements on Earth, would mean to the man or men who could control them. Here would be new sources of power greater than uranium, new properties as yet unknown to be explored and exploited from elements that had up to now been only the expensive toys of laboratory researchers. Perhaps, even, elements that hadn't been discovered or even guessed at yet . . .

By the time Comyn stepped out of the lift his brain was whirling with wild visions of atoms, electrons, and blazing bursts of power that paled the Sun. They were vague, but immensely impressive. They frightened him.

He picked up his customary shadow outside the building, and, under cover of lighting a cigarette, looked around for the other one. This second watcher was more careful and expert than the first, who did not seem to care much whether Comyn saw him or not. If it hadn't been for that accident of reflection, Comyn would probably never have noticed him.

As it was, he had to let three matches blow out before he spotted the man again, a tall slightly stooping figure in a gray suit. Comyn couldn't see his face, but something about the set and stance of him sent that cold flash up his spine again. Comyn didn't know nuclear physics, but he knew men. This one meant business.

Was he the stand-by, the hatchet-man sent along by the Cochranes in case things got beyond the capabilities of the mild-faced individual who seemed only to be doing a not-too-interesting job? Or had somebody else dealt himself a hand in the game?

Transuranic, whispered Ballantyne's ghostly voice in his ear. *Transuranic*—the echo of a scream.

There was a bar on the corner and Comyn made for it. A couple of stiff ones stopped his insides from shaking. He switched to beer because he thought better on it, and went back to his brooding. He had found a place in the corner where nobody could get behind him. The bar was crowded, but even so he could see his twin satellites. They were behaving like casual customers, apparently unaware of him and of each other.

As he watched them through the haze of smoke, the din of voices and the yeasty stirring of the crowd, he grew certain of one thing. The mild-faced man *was* unaware of the other one. If the Cochranes had sent him along for the dirty work, they hadn't told their other boy anything about it.

The afternoon wore away. The big videoscreen at the end of the bar poured out a steady stream of speeches, special bulletins, rehashes and fresh opinions about the Big

Jump. The crowd picked them up, chewed them over, argued and chattered and had another drink. Comyn stared gloomily at the bubbles rising in his glass.

It became evening . . . and then night. The crowd changed constantly, but Comyn was still there, and so were the two men: the mild-faced gent in the rumpled jacket, and the other one who was not mild. Comyn had drunk a lot of beer by now and done a lot of thinking. He was watching the men and there was a curiously bright glint in his eye.

The name of Cochrane sounded over and over from the screen, as often as the name of Ballantyne. It began to prick a nerve in Comyn, a nerve connected with whatever center it was inside him that made hate.

"Mr. Jonas Cochrane, president of the Cochrane Corporation, today announced that his company would consider the Ballantyne star-drive as something to be held in trust for the good of all peoples . . ."

Comyn laughed into his beer. He could just imagine the old bandit sitting up in that fantastic castle on the Moon, thinking of the common good.

"The Cochrane Corporation has voted one hundred thousand dollars to the survivors of each of the five heroes of the first star-flight . . ."

Well, that was a nice gesture. Good publicity and deductible from income tax.

"Miss Sydna Cochrane has consented to say a few words about this historic achievement which her family helped to make possible. We switch you now to our on-the-spot reporter at the famous Rocket Room . . ."

The picture dissolved to the interior of a night club, furnished up in the style of such a ship as never sailed the seas of space. The camera focused in on a woman who was part of a group of expensively dressed young people being very gay at one of the tables. Comyn stared and forgot his beer.

She wore something white and severely plain that showed her off in exactly the right places, and it was all worth showing. Her skin was very brown, with the magnificent kind of tan you can only get from a lunar solarium. And her hair—probably bleached, Comyn thought, but damned effective

—was almost as light as her dress and was drawn straight to the back of her head, where it hung down in a thick hank as uncurled as combed flax. She had features that were bold and handsome and verging on the angular. Her mouth was wide, and her eyes were positively lambent. She was well geared, but held it like a man.

The voice of the announcer came over, trying to make his introduction heard above the noise. Miss Sydna Cochrane closed her strong brown hands around her champagne glass and leaned her brown and splendid shoulders almost into the lens. She smiled.

"Money," she said in a beautiful throaty voice, *"is only money. Without the courage and the genius of men like Ballantyne it accomplishes nothing. But I'm not going to talk about him. Millions of others are doing that. I'm going to talk about some other people that seem to have been more or less forgotten."*

Her eyes had an odd intensity, almost as though she were trying to see through the camera lens, through the screen, and find somebody. For some reason not associated with her low-cut gown, Comyn's pulses began to hammer strangely.

Her voice rolled out again. *"I'm going to talk about the four men who went with Ballantyne across the Big Jump, and died doing it. Not our money nor Ballantyne himself could have done anything without these four men."*

She lifted her champagne glass, in a gesture that could have been corny but was not.

"I'm going to drink to those four men: to Strang, Kessel, Vickery and—"

Was the pause deliberate, or was she just trying to remember the name? Her eyes were brilliant with some obscure deviltry.

"—and Paul Rogers. And I know at least one man who'll be glad to drink with me, if he's listening."

The mild-faced man started and glanced at Comyn in the bar mirror. The other one kept his eyes fastened on nothing, but his body moved on the stool with a slow snakelike undulation, and he smiled. Comyn's heart jolted and then ran on again with a fast steady beat. From that moment he knew exactly what he was going to do.

He didn't hurry. He didn't give any outward sign that he had heard Miss Sydna Cochrane or got her meaning. After a while he rose and went unsteadily into the washroom.

There was nobody in it. His unsteadiness disappeared. He flattened himself against the wall beside the door and waited. The one low window in the place was barred and there was no way out of it, but if he waited long enough the boys out there would get uneasy . . .

Footsteps came from outside, going slow. Then there was the absence of sound that meant somebody listening. Comyn held his breath. The door opened.

It was the harmless-looking gent in the rumpled jacket. Without malice, Comyn stepped forward and planted one on his jaw so swiftly that the man hardly had time to look surprised. Then Comyn tucked him away in a place ideally adapted for concealment. He risked a fast run-through of his pockets before he left him. The man's identification said his name was Lawrence Hannay and his occupation: operative for a well-known private detective agency. He carried no weapon.

Comyn went back and stood again beside the door.

This time he had a little longer to wait. A stranger came in and Comyn sweated blood until he left. Then there was silence again.

There was no sound of footsteps. The tall man walked silently. Comyn could feel him listening outside the door. Then it opened softly and slowly and the man came inside a step at a time, his left hand swinging free, his right hand in his pocket, his head hunched forward between his stooping shoulders.

Comyn slugged him hard behind the ear.

He twisted, as though the movement of air in front of Comyn's fist had been enough to warn him. The blow didn't hit square. He fell, still twisting, and Comyn threw himself aside. Something made a tiny shrilling sound like an insect going past him and snicked against the tiled wall. Comyn sprang.

The man was only half stunned. His body whipped and writhed under Comyn's knees and his breath hissed. He had a narrow face and a bristle of rusty hair, and the teeth he sank into Comyn's wrist were brown and bad. He wanted hard to get his right hand up so he could shoot his little toy into Comyn without any danger of hitting himself. But Comyn was kneeling on it, crushing it down into the man's own belly, and both of them knew better than to let go. Comyn grunted and his fist went up and down two or three times. The narrow skull cracked audibly on the tile floor. After the third time the man relaxed.

Comyn sat him against the wall with his head bent over his knees, in the attitude of a drunk who has passed out. With great care he took the small ugly weapon out of his pocket. It was one of the kind Comyn had threatened the guard with on Mars, and he thought how glad that guard would be to know that he had been shot at with it. He dropped it in the wastebasket under a drift of paper towels. Then he searched the man.

There was nothing on him: not a card, not a name. He was a careful man.

Comyn filled his cupped hands with cold water and threw it in the man's face. Then he slapped him. Eyes opened, narrow and colorless under rusty brows, and looked into Comyn's face.

"You're no private op. Who are you?"

Three short unhelpful words.

Comyn hit him again. He had been on the receiving end himself for the Cochranes, and it gave him a certain pleasure to be handing it back to someone.

"Come on, buster. Who hired you to kill me?"

Comyn lifted his hand again, and the man showed his brown and broken teeth.

"Go ahead," he said. "See if you can make me."

Comyn considered him. "It would be a lot of fun, but the lady won't wait all night. And this isn't exactly the place for that kind of a talk, either." He showed his own teeth. "Anyway, you'll have a nice time explaining to your boss just why you didn't earn his money."

"I'll be back. I got a reason now."

"Aw," said Comyn, "I've made you real mad—just because I wouldn't stand still! Isn't that too bad." He hauled back his fist and let it go with deliberate and vicious intent.

The man folded up quietly against the wall. Comyn went out, paid his check in the bar and left. This time he was not followed by anybody.

He found a cab and headed for the Rocket Room. He wondered about two things as he rode. The first was whether Miss Sydna Cochrane had chosen a rather peculiar way of giving the signal to have him finished off. The second was whether her legs would measure up to the rest of her. He rather thought they would.

IV

THERE were nine pretty little worlds that moved slowly around the softly glowing orb of their Sun. They moved quite silently in the ceiling, but you couldn't have heard them anyway, so loud was the buzz in the Rocket Room.

And the buzz of voices had the one name all through it, the same as everywhere. Comyn got it all the way, from the men and women at the shimmering bar that had real pilot-seats and a phony space-window instead of a mirror, and from the crowded tables he passed.

He thought of a screaming man, and wondered bitterly, *Are you happy, Ballantyne? You made the Big Jump and you died, but you're a hero to all these people. Wasn't it worth it?*

The waiter who happened into Comyn's path asked deferentially, "Did you want to see someone at Miss Cochrane's table, sir?"

But it wasn't a waiter, not a real one. When Comyn looked closer, he knew this man hadn't just happened.

Comyn said wearily, "Yes, I do. Can you take that to the Crown Princess yourself, or does it have to go through the captain of the guard?"

The waiter examined him, without seeming to. "It would depend . . ."

"Yeah. Well, ask her if she still wants to drink to Paul Rogers."

The waiter glanced at him sharply. "Your name is . . . ?"

"Comyn."

"You're expected, Mr. Comyn."

He turned and led the way to the big table that was apparently in the best position in the place. It was the one Comyn had been making for when he was stopped. Miss Sydna Cochrane watched them come.

The man who was pretending to be a waiter spoke to her, received a nod and went back to his post. She leaned back in her chair, showing the fine strong lines of her throat and breast, and smiled up at Comyn. She had had a few more champagnes since he saw her on the videocast, but she was still holding them well.

"So!" she said. "You look like the type that could do it, all right. Would it please you to know that you've still got 'em spinning?"

"Who?"

"The Cochranes. Round and round." She described circles with her forefinger. "All except me, of course. Sit down. Make yourself at home."

Chair, glass, champagne and genuine waiter had appeared like magic. Comyn sat. The dozen or so others at the table were chattering like magpies, demanding to be told who Comyn was and what the mystery was all about. Sydna ignored them. The tall willowy boy who sat on her left peered across her shoulder and glowered. She ignored him, too.

"Pretty clever of me, I thought. That spur-of-the-minute speech, I mean."

"Real cute, Miss Cochrane. So cute it nearly got me killed."

"What?"

"Five minutes after you made that crack about Paul Rogers somebody took a shot at me."

She frowned and a shadow of some dark thought he couldn't read came into her eyes.

"Was that your idea?" he asked her softly.

"My friend," she said, "they shoved a camera in my face, and I spoke. Even in this modern age there are thousands of places that don't have videos. You might have been in any one of them." She began to get her temper up. "And furthermore, if you think—"

"Whoa!" he said, and grinned. "Okay. I take it back. What about that drink?"

She continued to stare at him, her red mouth set and sulky, her brows drawn down. The clamor had now become deafening around the table. Comyn leaned back, rolling the stemmed glass slowly between his hands, not thinking about it, looking at the white dress and what it covered, and what it didn't cover, letting her take her time. He was in no hurry. He could look at that all night.

The anger went out of her eyes, leaving them lazy and full of sparks. "I'm not sure I'm going to like you," she said, "but I'm willing to find out. Come on."

· She uncoiled out of the chair, and Comyn rose with her. In her high heels she stood as tall as he did. "Where are we going?" he asked.

"Who knows? Maybe the Moon." She laughed and waved to her guests, who were protesting violently. "You're lovely people, but you make too much noise. 'Bye."

The willowy lad sprang up. "Now see here, Sydna," he said angrily, "I'm your escort and I won't have—"

"Johnny."

"You can't just go off with this—this character in the middle of the night! It isn't—"

"Johnny," said Sydna, "you're a nice boy, but Comyn can lick you. And if you don't stop minding my business I'll have him do it." She touched Comyn's arm and swept on ahead of him, walking with a long arrogant stride that even the high heels couldn't ruin. Comyn followed her, anxious to get away from the red-faced Johnny before he had to make good on Sydna's promise whether he wanted to or not.

Her back, bare to the waist, was brown as a copper penny and the hank of flaxen hair swung against it. Comyn watched the smooth play of muscles up and down that back as she walked. He thought that she could probably have licked the kid herself, without help. Quite a dame.

He settled down beside her on the cushions of a limousine that arrived at the door almost as soon as they did. He turned a little sideways so he could see her.

"Well," he said, "what now?"

She crossed her knees, burrowed her head back into the cushions and yawned like a cat. "I haven't decided yet."

The chauffeur, apparently accustomed to such vagaries, began to drive slowly along, going nowhere in particular. Sydna lay back in her corner and watched Comyn from under half-closed lids. The flicker of passing lights gleamed on her white dress, touched her hair, her mouth, the angle of a cheekbone.

"I'm sleepy," she said.

"Too sleepy to tell me what you wanted with me?"

"Curiosity. Wanted to see the man the Cochranes couldn't keep out." She smiled with sudden malice. "I wanted to see the man that got Willy in dutch."

"Who's Willy?"

"My little cousin's beloved husband. Stanley." She leaned forward. "Do you like Stanley?"

"I can't say I'm bursting over with affection for him."

"He's a louse," said Sydna, and relaxed again into the upholstery, brooding. Then she clicked open the communicator. "I've decided," she said. "Take us to the spaceport."

"Yes, Miss Cochrane," said the chauffeur, stifling a yawn, and the communicator snapped shut again.

"Us?" said Comyn.

"I told you maybe we'd go to the Moon."

"Don't I have a choice in the matter?"

"Don't kid me, Comyn. Right in the middle of the Cochrane stronghold? You're crazy to get there."

He leaned over her, putting his hand on the smooth ridge of muscles where her neck curved into her shoulder. It quivered slightly, and he tightened his fingers.

"I don't like having my mind made up for me," he said. "Not too fast."

"Neither do I," said Sydna, and put her hands up alongside his head. Her nails bit suddenly into the flesh behind his ears, pulling his head down. She was laughing.

After a while he straightened up and said, "You play rough."

"I grew up with three brothers. I had to play rough or not play."

They looked at each other in the half dark; they were hot-eyed, bristling, between anger and excitement. Then she said slowly, almost viciously:

"You'll come because there's something up there you'll want to see."

"What?"

She didn't answer. Quite suddenly, she had begun to shiver, her hands clasped tight together in her lap.

"Buy me a drink, Comyn."

"Haven't you had enough?"

"There isn't enough in New York."

"What have you people got now, up there on the Moon?"

"Progress. Expansion. Glory. The stars." She swore, still quivering. "Why did Ballantyne have to make his damned trip, Comyn? Weren't nine worlds enough room to make trouble in? Trouble. That's what we've got up there. That's why I came to Earth."

She lifted those wide brown shoulders and let them fall. "I'm a Cochrane and I'm stuck with it." She paused, looking at Comyn. "So are you—stuck with it, I mean. Would you rather be on the outside, getting shot at—or on the inside?"

"Getting shot at?"

"I can't guarantee you anything."

"Hm."

"Oh, run away if you want to, Comyn." She had got over her shakes, and he wondered if the champagne might not have been responsible for them. It seemed to be coming over her in a wave now. Or else she was taking that way to duck any more questions. "I'm sleepy. I don't care what you do."

And she went to sleep, or seemed to, with her head against him and his arm around her. She was no lightweight, but the long lithe curves of her body were pleasant to follow. He held them, thinking of all the many ways in which this might be a trap. Or was Miss Sydna Cochrane just a little crazy? They said all the Cochranes were a little crazy; they'd been saying that ever since old Jonas had built the ridiculous lunar palace toward which he was now heading.

The car was bearing them on toward the spaceport. He could still back out, but he'd have to do it fast.

No. I can't back out, thought Comyn. *Not now.*

He had only one chance to find out about Paul Rogers, and that was to bluff information out of the Cochranes—if he could. He also only had one chance to maybe get himself on a little solider ground, and that was by the same method. He would never get a better crack at trying.

A hard-boiled little lamb going to talk a lot of lions out of their dinner, Comyn told himself grimly. *Oh, well, if I'm stepping into it, it's in nice company.*

He settled back, patting Miss Cochrane into a more comfortable position, and wished he knew two things: who had paid the boy with the bad teeth to kill him, and whether this ace in the hole he was going to bluff the Cochranes with might not turn out to be just a low spade after all—a spade suitable for grave digging.

They went through the spaceport and into the glittering Cochrane yacht, as though through a well-oiled machine. When the yacht had cleared, Sydna went sleepily away to change and left Comyn staring with increasing distaste at the blank, enlarging lunar face ahead.

Why the devil would anyone want to build a showplace out on this skull's head? They said old Jonas had done it so that the Cochrane wealth and power would be forever in the eyes of all Earth, and that he rarely left it. The old pirate must have a screw loose.

The yacht swept in toward the Lunar Appenines, showing a magnificent view of the sharp and towering peaks in the full blaze of day. Luna, he thought, could still beat anything in the Solar System for sheer scenery, if your nerves could stand it. The great ringed plain Archimedes showed its encircling fangs far off to the left, and ahead, on a plateau halfway up that naked mountain wall, he caught a flash of reflected sunlight.

"That's the dome," said Sydna. "We're almost there."

She didn't sound happy about it. Comyn glanced at her. She had finally come back, wearing white slacks and a silk shirt. She was still fixing her make-up.

"If you don't like the place, why do you ever go there?" he asked.

She shrugged. "Jonas won't leave it. And we have to show up every so often. He's still head of the family."

Comyn looked at her more closely. "You're scared," he said. "Scared of something up here."

She laughed. "I don't scare easy."

"I believe that," he said. "But you're afraid now. Of what?

Why did you run away from here to New York to get tight?"

She looked at him somberly. "Maybe you're about to find out. Or maybe I'm just leading you to the slaughter."

He put his hands up on either side of her neck, not tenderly.

"Are you?"

"Could be, Comyn."

"I've got a feeling," he said, "that one of these days I'll be sorry I didn't break this for you right here."

"We may both be," she said, and then surprised him when he kissed her, for there was panic in the way she pressed against him.

He didn't like it at all, and he liked the whole thing less and less as the yacht swooped smoothly down to that high plateau above the Mare Imbrium. He saw the curve of the enormous pressure dome rising up like a smooth glass mountain flashing in the sun, and then a magnetic tug had hooked onto their ship and they were being handled smoothly into an airlock. Massive doors closed behind them, and Comyn thought, *Well, here I am—and it's up to the Cochranes whether I ever leave or not.*

A few minutes later he was driving with Sydna through rioting gardens that covered several acres, toward a pile of masonry he had seen pictured many times before: an old man's arrogant monument to himself, insanely set upon a dead world. The stark structure of native lunar rock had been designed by a master architect to match the lunar landscape. The result was striking, weird—and, he had to admit, beautiful. The lines of the buildings lifted and swept and curved as boldly as the peaks that loomed above them.

He followed Sydna out and went up some broad and shallow steps to a portico of tremendous simplicity. Sydna pushed open the great doors that were made of a dully-gleaming alloy.

The hall inside was high and austere, flooded with filtered lunar sunlight, and softened with hangings, rugs and a few priceless oddments from all over the Solar System. The vault of white stone flung back a whispering echo as they moved. Sydna walked halfway along its length, going slower and slower. Then she turned suddenly around as though she wanted to run back. Comyn took her by the shoulder and asked again:

"What are you afraid of? I want to know!"

The echoes of his voice whispered back and forth between the walls. She shrugged, not looking at him, trying to keep her voice light.

"Don't you know every castle has a Thing living in its cellar? Well, we've got one here too, now, and it's a beaut."

"What kind of a thing?" demanded Comyn.

"I think," said Sydna, "I think . . . it's Ballantyne."

V

THE HIGH vault muttered *Ballantyne* in a thousand tiny voices, and Comyn's grip had become a painful thing on Sydna's shoulders.

"What do you mean, it's Ballantyne? He's dead; I saw him die!"

Sydna's eyes met his now, steadily, for a long minute, and it seemed to Comyn that a cold wind blew in that closed place, cold as the spaces between the stars.

"They haven't let me go down there," she said, "and they won't talk to me about it, but you can't keep any secrets here. The echoes are too good. And I can tell you another thing. I'm not the only one that's scared."

Something caught hold of Comyn's heart and began to shake it. Sydna's face turned indistinct and distant and he was back again in a little room on Mars, looking at the shadow of a fear that was new under the familiar Sun . . .

"Surprise," said Sydna, in a cool light voice with barbs on it. "I've brought a friend of yours."

Comyn started and turned. William Stanley was standing in the doorway at the far end of the hall, a smile of welcome turning dark and ugly on his face. Comyn took his hands away from Sydna.

Stanley shot him one blazing look and then turned on Sydna. "Of all the hen-brained female tricks! What does it take to make you grow up, Sydna? The end of the world?"

"Why, Willy!" She looked at him in innocent amazement. "Did I do wrong?"

Stanley's face was now absolutely white. "No," he said, answering his own question and not hers, "not even the end of the world would do it. You'd still be busy impressing everyone with how devastatingly cute you are. But I don't think that anybody is going to find this one the least bit funny." He jerked his head at Comyn. "Turn around. You're going back to Earth."

Sydna was smiling, but her eyes had that lambency that Comyn remembered. She seemed to be much interested in Stanley. "Say that over again. That last bit."

Stanley repeated slowly. "I said, this man is going back to Earth."

Sydna nodded. "You're getting better at it, Willy, but you're still not good enough."

"Good enough at what?"

"Giving orders like a Cochrane." She turned her back on him, not insultingly but as though he just wasn't there.

In a voice that had trouble getting out, Stanley said, "We'll see about this."

He strode away. Sydna did not look after him. Neither did Comyn. He had forgotten Stanley after the first minute. *I think—I think it's Ballantyne.* How long could a thing go on, how ugly could it get?

He demanded harshly, "Just what are you trying to give me?"

"It's hard to take, isn't it? Maybe you know now why I went down to New York."

"Listen," said Comyn. "I was with Ballantyne. His heart had stopped. They tried to get it going again, but it was no use. I saw him. He was dead."

"Yes," said Sydna, "I know. That's what makes it so sticky. His heart's still stopped. He's dead, but not quite."

Comyn swore at her with a savagery born of fear. "How can a man be dead, and— How do you know? You said you hadn't been let down to see him. How—"

"She listens at keyholes," said a new voice. A man was coming down the hall toward them, his heels clicking angrily on the stone floor. "Listens," he said, "and then talks. Can't you ever learn to keep your mouth shut? Can't you ever stop making trouble?"

His face was Sydna's face all over again but it was without the beauty, high-boned and dark. His eyes had the same brightness, but it was a cruel thing now, and the lines around his mouth were deep. He looked as though he wanted to take Sydna in his two hands and break her.

She didn't give any ground. "Throwing a tantrum isn't going to change things, Pete, so you might as well not."

Her own eyes had fired up, and her mouth was stubborn. "Comyn, this is Peter Cochrane, my brother. Pete, this is . . ."

The bitter dark eyes flicked briefly over Comyn. "I know, I've seen him before." He returned his attention to Sydna. Somewhere from the background Stanley spoke, reiterating his demand that Comyn be sent away. Nobody noticed him. Comyn said:

"Where?"

"On Mars. You wouldn't remember. You weren't feeling well at the time."

A vague memory of a voice speaking beyond a thick red haze returned to Comyn. "So it was you who broke up the party."

"The boys were enjoying their work too much. You were liable to be ruined before you talked." He swung around on Comyn. "Are you ready to talk now?"

Comyn stepped closer to him. "Is Ballantyne dead?"

Peter Cochrane hesitated. The wire-drawn look deepened, and a muscle began to twitch under his cheekbone. "You and your big mouth," he muttered to Sydna. "You—"

"All right," she answered furiously, "so you're mad. The hell with you. You and the whole Cochrane tribe aren't getting anywhere on this, and you know it. I thought Comyn might have the answer.

Comyn repeated, "Is Ballantyne dead?"

Peter said, after a moment, "I don't know."

Comyn closed his fists hard and took a deep breath. "Let's put it another way, then. Dead or alive, I want to see him."

"No. No, you don't—but you won't know it till afterward." He studied Comyn with a hard penetrating look. "What are you after, Comyn? A chance to cut in?"

Comyn gestured toward Stanley. "I told him, already. I told your boys on Mars. I want to find out what happened to Paul Rogers."

"Just a noble sentiment of friendship? It's too thin, Comyn."

"More than just friendship," Comyn said. "Paul Rogers saved my neck, once. He went to bat for me out on Ganymede when he didn't have to. I'll tell you about it sometime. The point is, I like to pay my debts. I'm going to find out about him if I have to blow the Cochranes wide open."

"You don't, I take it, like the Cochranes?"

Comyn said savagely, "Who does? And you're running true to form now, kicking Ballantyne around like a football, snatching his ship, holding out the log books, trying to sew up the Big Jump—the biggest thing men ever did—like any cheap swindling business deal."

"Let's get things straight," interrupted Peter harshly. "That ship and its star-drive belong to us. And the log broke off just where we said. And we brought Ballantyne here to try to do something for him, about him—" He broke off, his face quivering slightly as though in involuntary recoil from some shocking memory.

Comyn felt the chill shadow of the other's emotion, but he said again, "Are you going to let me see him?"

"Why should I? Why shouldn't I just send you back to Earth?"

"Because," Comyn said grimly, "you know I know something, and you want to know what."

"He doesn't know anything!" Stanley exclaimed to Peter. "How could he? Ballantyne was in terminal coma and couldn't talk. He's bluffing, trying to chisel in."

"Maybe," said Peter Cochrane. "We'll find out. All right, Comyn. You convince me you know something, and you can see Ballantyne. But I'm making no deals with you beyond that. I'm only one Cochrane, and this concerns all of us. The others won't be here until this evening, Earth time, and we can fight it out then. Fair enough?"

Comyn nodded. "Fair enough."

"Then, what *do* you know?"

"Not a lot," said Comyn. It was time for his one little card, and he had to play it as casually as though he had a fistful behind it. "Not a lot. But I do know there'd be quite a bit of excitement if people thought there was a transuranic world out there."

There was a moment of silence. Peter Cochrane did not change expression, but the color drained slowly out of Stanley's face, leaving it gray. Then Sydna spoke into the silence.

"He did know. And that's why somebody tried to kill him."

Peter Cochrane looked at her sharply. "That's ridiculous. He wouldn't be worth a nickel to anybody dead."

"Do I get to see Ballantyne now?" Comyn demanded.

Cochrane turned abruptly. "Yes. You've asked for it. Sydna, you stay here. You've made enough trouble for one day."

"I have every intention of staying here, and I need a drink!" she said.

Comyn followed Peter Cochrane down the corridor. Stanley went with them. There was a sliding metal door at the end of the corridor, and behind it there was a lift that sank downward into the lunar rock, whining softly. Comyn had begun to sweat, and his shirt stuck to him, coldly damp across his back. His heart was pounding, not steadily, but in irregular bursts that made it hard to breathe. The lines in Peter Cochrane's face were deep. He looked as though he hadn't slept for some time. Stanley stood apart from them, withdrawn into his own thoughts. His eyes moved constantly from Comyn to Peter Cochrane and back again. A ridge of muscle showed along his jaw.

The lift stopped and they got out. There was nothing mysterious about these cellars under the Cochrane castle. They held the pumping plants for air and water, the generators, the mountainous quantities of supplies necessary for maintaining life and luxury in this artificial blister on the face of Luna. The rock floor they walked on quivered to the rhythmic throbbing of the pumps.

Cochrane moved like a man who was being forced to witness an execution. Comyn thought the man had probably been this way before too often, and he caught the subtle contagion of dread from the dark strained face. Stanley lagged behind them both, his feet scuffing on the smooth rock.

Peter Cochrane paused before a door. He didn't look at anyone. He said, "Why don't you stay out here, Bill?"

Stanley said, "No."

Comyn's mouth was dry. There was an acrid taste in it, and his nerve ends hurt.

Peter Cochrane still hesitated, scowling at his hand as he put it up against the door.

Comyn said, "Come on, come on!" His voice came out rough and no louder than a whisper.

Cochrane pushed the door open.

There was a room cut out of the rock. It had been hastily cleared of most of the stores that had been in it, and just as hastily fitted up with things that made it partly a laboratory, partly a hospital, and partly a cell. Strong lights filled it with a naked and pitiless glare. There were two men in it—and something else.

Comyn recognized the young doctor from the hospital on Mars. He had lost much of his youth. The other man he didn't know, but the same look of strain and dread was on him. They turned around with the violence that came of overtaxed nerves. They had been startled by the opening of the door. The young doctor looked at Comyn, and his eyes got wide.

"You again," he said. "How did you—"

"Never mind that," said Cochrane swiftly. He kept his gaze on the doctor, on the floor, anywhere but on the white bed with the siderails up on it. "Is there any change?"

Things were fading out for Comyn. He had taken a few steps forward, drawn by that white barred oblong beyond the two men, beyond the apparatus and the laboratory benches. The light was very brilliant, very clear. It was focused now upon the bed, and around it things seemed to be fading out: the men, the voices, the emotions.

Far off on another world the doctor was saying, "No change. Roth and I have completed . . ."

No. It was bad enough on Mars. I heard him scream and I saw him die, and that was bad enough. Nobody ought to have to look at this.

A voice, another one. "I told you before what my findings were. I've verified them, as far as anybody can. I can't go beyond the limits of my equipment. This has got to wait for a whole new science." Excitement in the voice, stronger than dread, stronger than anything.

"I know that, Roth. I know it."

Voices, men, tension, fear—going round, going faster, dissolving in a darkening mist around that single intense point of light. Comyn put out his hands, not knowing that he did it, and took hold of the cold top bar of the bed. He hung on while the warmth and the strength drained out of him and left him empty of everything but a sickening horror.

The thing that lay in the bed between the barred sides was Ballantyne. It was Ballantyne, and it was dead, quite dead. There was no covering on it to hide its deadness; no breathing lifted the flattened ribs; no pulse beat anywhere beneath the pale transparent skin, and the tracery of veins was dark, and the face was . . .

Dead. And yet—it moved.

The faint unceasing twitchings and drawings of the flesh that Comyn remembered when Ballantyne was still alive had increased and taken over now that he was dead. It was as though some new and dreadful form of life had claimed the wasted shell when Ballantyne had left it: a brainless, blind, insensate life that only knew to move, to stir and pluck the strings of muscles that lifted the skeletal limbs and put them down again, that made the fingers grasp and close and the head turn slowly from side to side.

It was motion without reason, without sound except for the rustling of the sheet. Motion that laid a blasphemous hand even on the face that had no longer any thought or being behind it, and made it . . .

Comyn heard a hoarse and distant sound. It was himself trying to speak and not making it. He let go of the bed. After that he didn't hear or see anything until he fetched up against some solid object with a crash that knocked some sense back into him. He stood where he was, shaking all over, the breath coming raw and rasping into his throat. Gradually the room stopped swinging and he was able to think again.

Peter Cochrane said, "You wanted to come."

Comyn didn't answer. He moved away from the bed, as fast as he could get, and kept his back to it. He could still hear the dry vague rustling that never stopped.

Cochrane turned to the doctor. "What I want to know for sure," he said, "is this: could Ballantyne ever—ever *live* again? As Ballantyne, I mean. As a human being."

The doctor made a decisive gesture. "No. Ballantyne died, from heart failure due to exhaustion. He is dead, by every normal physiologic standard. His brain is already deteriorating. But his body has in it a residue of some weird new physiological activity—I can hardly call it life."

"What kind of activity? We're not scientists, doctor."

The other hesitated. "The ordinary processes of metabolism ceased in Ballantyne's body cells when he died. But there's a residual process that keeps going on. And it's something brand new. It's a low-level flow of energy in the cells, not generated by the usual biochemical metabolic process, but by the slow degeneration of certain transuranic elements."

Comyn looked up sharply.

"You mean," Cochrane was saying slowly, "he has suffered a kind of radioactive poisoning?"

The doctor shook his head, and Roth said firmly, "No, this is definitely not toxic radioactivity. The elements that Ballantyne's body cells absorbed are beyond the range of our chemistry, even of the transuranic chemistry our labs have been dabbling with. They don't emit injurious radiation, but do release energy."

They glanced briefly and against their will at the bed, and Cochrane said somberly, "Then his . . . movements . . . are merely a mechanical reflex?"

The doctor nodded. "Yes. The cytoplasm of the contractile-tissue cells, such as the muscle fibres, is constantly activated by the flow of energy."

"But he's really dead?"

"Yes. He's dead."

Stanley broke into the brooding moment of silence that followed. "What are we going to do with him? We can't let people see him. There'd be an uproar, an examination, and it would all be out!"

"No, we can't let people see him," Cochrane agreed slowly. He said, after a moment, to Stanley. "You get the Earth news-services on the phone. Tell them that we're going to give Ballantyne the hero's funeral he deserves—and one that all Earth can see."

"All Earth? Peter, you're crazy—"

"Am I? Maybe. Anyway, Ballantyne had no close family

so nobody can stop us. Tell them to watch the northwest corner of Mare Imbrium in an hour."

Comyn got it, then. He exhaled a long breath. Cochrane glanced at him briefly, and then once more at the barred unquiet bed.

"I know how you feel," he said. "Besides, he's come a long way. He deserves to rest."

They went out then, back up into the light, into the cooled and freshened air, and the scent of flowers that came in from the rioting gardens. And in Comyn's mind that faint remembered voice was whispering, *Oh God, why did it have to be transuranic . . .* And he was sick, with a sickness that he thought would never leave him while he lived.

Sydna was waiting. Cochrane and Stanley were busy now with this thing they were about to do. They hardly noticed when she took Comyn by the arm and led him off, out to a terrace above the gardens where the filtered sunlight poured down fiercely and took some of the coldness out of his bones. She put a drink in his hands and waited, looking at his face, until he noticed her and began to speak.

"Don't tell me about it," she said sharply. "No."

After a moment she drew closer to him and murmured, "Don't look startled or surprised. They can see us from the windows. Comyn, will you leave here now? I can still get you away."

He looked down at her. "What's the matter?"

"You were down there a long time. The family has started to arrive. Comyn—"

"You've had a few."

"And I wish I'd had more! Listen, I got you into this. I blew my top about Ballantyne and brought you up here. I'm trying to get you out while I can still do it."

His eyes were bleak. "Afraid I *am* trying to cut in on the profits?"

"You bloody fool! You don't know us Cochranes. This thing is big, and that means people are going to get hurt. Will you go?"

Comyn shook his head. "I can't."

She looked at him, narrow-eyed, and then she said mercilessly, "Are you sure now you *want* to find your friend Paul Rogers?"

Comyn was glad he did not have to answer that question, right now. For at the moment, from the terrace they saw the sleek, purring, airtight truck heading away from the mansion and going toward the lock.

They watched it in silence as it went out of the dome and down the ledges, back and forth, onto the great lunar plain. It went so far out on the plain that it was but a dot. It stayed there a while and then came back.

Then, for them and for all watching Earth to see, upon the Mare Imbrium flared a dazzling flower of atomic flame—blazing, soaring, and then dying away. A hero's funeral pyre, with a world for witness. Comyn unclenched his hands. And Sydna slipped something into one of them.

It was a shocker, still warm from her body. She said, "All right, come on and meet my family."

VI

IT WAS THE most ridiculous room he had ever seen. It was comparatively small, and it was furnished in the overstuffed fashion of three generations before. It had a long, shabby sofa, lumpish chairs and drifts of small tables. One wall was filter-glass, but the other walls were covered with incongruous flowered wallpaper. And there was a fireplace with a mantel above it—a fireplace here in this super-modern castle on the Moon!

Six or seven people sat about the room, but when Comyn came in with Sydna they stopped talking and stared at him. He felt as if he were walking into an ambush of hostile eyes. Stanley was sitting in a corner beside one of those muffin-faced girls that, sooner or later, happened to every family. Beyond him, by the fireplace, was a shabby Morris chair. The figure seated in it was the focus of the whole room.

"This is the man, Grandfather," said Peter Cochrane. The burst of atomic fire out on the Mare Imbrium seemed to have burned something out of him. He had the look of one exhausted by grappling with the impossible.

A voice spoke out of the old Morris chair. "You," it said. "Come here."

Comyn went and looked down at the old, old man who sat in the chair watching him with eyes like two dark glowing embers.

He said, "You're Jonas Cochrane."

The old face, seamed and shrivelled and shrunken tight over the characteristic jutting bones, was stamped with a long lifetime of acquired wisdom, none of it saintly. Only that face made it possible to identify this ancient man—wrapped in a shabby woolen robe and dusted with cigarette ash—with the crafty, ruthless schemer of the old days who had clawed top place for his family in the great game of ships and planets.

Over his head on the mantel, amid a grotesque ruck of mementos—of baby shoes preserved in bronze, models of the first Cochrane flagships, faded photographs of prosaic Middle-Western houses and people—Jonas Cochrane's face was startlingly repeated in a well-done miniature of a Sioux Indian chief.

"That's Old-Man-Afraid-Of-His-Horses," said Jonas, with pride. "On the mother's side, I'm a direct descendant." He went on, without any change of tone, "I don't like interference, especially from amateurs. They're unpredictable. You've made us a lot of trouble, Comyn."

"Enough trouble," asked Comyn softly, "that you decided to have me killed?"

Jonas Cochrane's eyes grew narrow and very bright. "Murder is for fools," he said. "I've never indulged in it. What are you talking about?"

Comyn told him.

Jonas leaned forward, looking past Comyn. "Are any of you responsible for this? Peter?"

Peter snapped, "Of course not. I'll get hold of Hannay."

He went out. A couple more people had come in by now, and Comyn thought he could place them: Sydna's other two brothers, one strongly resembling Peter but without the iron in him, the other fairer and more round-faced, with a merry, self-indulgent look. There was a gray-haired man with a mouth like a steel trap and a chronically ill-tempered expression, and Comyn knew he was the survivor of Jonas' two sons. He could guess the reason for the sour disposition. Old Jonas had lived too long.

There were some other third-generation Cochranes, male and female, including the girl who was sitting with Stanley, looking from him to the others with vague alarm, and sneaking glances at Comyn as though he might suddenly go off like a bomb. That would be Sydna's cousin. Stanley did not seem much relieved by the disposal of Ballantyne. He sat staring at his feet, snarling occasionally in a genteel way when his wife whispered to him.

Beside them was a middle-aged-to-elderly woman who looked more like Old-Man-Afraid-Of-His-Horses than Jonas did, except that the Sioux chief had a far kindlier face.

She looked impatient, and said sharply, "Father, why are we wasting time on this person? I've come all the way up here to discuss business, and I don't see any reason—"

"Of course you don't," said Jonas tartly. "You're a fool. You always were a fool, Sally. Just sit there and don't bother me."

Somebody snickered. Jonas' daughter sprang up. "Father or no father, I don't have to take that kind of talk! And I won't. I . . ."

Jonas, ignoring her splutter, lighted a cigarette with large hands that were so weak they trembled with the effort. Everyone else seemed amused, except Muffin-face, who looked distressed.

"Don't you mind, Mother," she whispered timidly.

Jonas regarded them both with a great weariness, "Women," he said.

Peter Cochrane came back. "Well, Comyn, Hannay says you slugged him and parked him in the washroom, and that's all he knows. He didn't see anyone else following you, nor did he see any attack."

Comyn shrugged. "He wouldn't. He was out cold. And the other guy was much better at tailing than Hannay."

Stanley said, "We've only Comyn's word that he ever was attacked."

"And, Comyn," said Peter, "you hadn't tried to negotiate with anyone, so who would want to silence you? You could have some personal enemies—"

"Sure," said Comyn. "But this wasn't one of them. And they don't hate me that bad."

Stanley shrugged. "How do you know? Anyway, I can't see that it's very important, except to you."

"Oh, but it is," said old Jonas softly. "You're a fool too, Stanley, or you'd see it. If he's telling the truth, it means that somebody didn't want him to talk to the Cochranes. Somebody preferred to lose Comyn's possible knowledge rather than risk letting us have it. And that means—" He broke off, looking shrewdly at Comyn. "You have courage, but that's a cheap virtue. It's no good without brains. Have you got brains, too? Can you finish my line of reasoning?"

"Easy," Comyn answered. "You have been, or are about to be, double-crossed by somebody in your own camp."

There was an uproar of voices. Jonas' gray-haired son came to his feet and thrust his face close to Comyn's and shouted, "That statement alone brands you as a liar! No Cochrane would ever sell out!"

At that, Comyn laughed.

Peter's face had taken on a dark, savage look. "I'm afraid I agree with Uncle George. What Comyn implies would presuppose special knowledge on the traitor's part—something he knows that we don't know, that he was afraid Comyn might tell us. But there isn't any special knowledge. I examined Ballantyne's ship, the log, everything. And Stanley was with me, and Uncle George and Simon came almost at once."

"That's right," said the cheerful young man who was Peter's brother, and who was now more cheerful than he had any business to be. "We were all there together. And nobody else got aboard until we were through. No special knowledge for anybody. Wasn't any. Vouch for old Pete any time. Besides, it's silly. All Cochranes share and share alike."

He gave Comyn a slow, gliding look, and Comyn saw that underneath young Simon Cochrane was about as jovial as a cottonmouth.

"Personally," he said, "I don't give a damn one way or the other. I'm only interested in finding out whether Paul Rogers is alive or not, and bringing him back safe if he is." He faced old Jonas squarely. "There's going to be a second Big Jump. I want to go along."

And that was it. It was funny, he thought, how you kept a crazy idea in your mind, how you told yourself it was crazy and not a thing you'd ever do, and then sudddenly you said, "I want to go along," and you knew that all the time you'd been planning to do it.

Peter Cochrane said angrily, "You go? What are you, Comyn—the White Knight? If Rogers or any of the other three are alive, we'll bring them back."

Comyn shook his head. "No dice. The Cochranes have always liked a clear field, and this one is too easy to sweep clean. To put it crudely, I don't trust you."

An uproar of voices began, with Sally Cochrane's shrill indignant trumpeting rising above the rest. Old Jonas held up his hand.

"Quiet," he said. "All of you!" He looked up into Comyn's face with eyes very bright, very hard, as ruthless as an old eagle's. "You'll have to pay for what you want, Comyn. Pay high."

"Yeah."

The room had become quite still. The light clinking of bracelets was clearly audible as Sally Cochrane leaned forward. They all leaned forward, intent on Comyn and the old man, intent on every word.

Jonas said, "Ballantyne talked before he . . . died."

"He talked."

"But how much, Comyn? How much? Transuranic isn't enough." Jonas hitched himself upward in the chair. He was a gaunt rack of bones with the hot pleasure of combat still burning in it. "And don't try to blackmail me, Comyn. Don't threaten me with United Tradelines or anyone else. You're here under a glass bubble on the Moon and you can't get out. Understand that? You're here for as long as it suits me, and you can't talk to anyone. This place has come in handy that way before. Now, go on."

There was silence in the room—a silence of held breath, and hostile faces flushed and watching. The palms of Comyn's hands were wet. He was walking a thin wire, and one wrong step would be enough.

"No," said Comyn slowly, "transuranic isn't enough now. You got that much from Ballantyne's own body cells. But there was more."

Silence. A ring of eyes around him, hot and hungry, eager and cruel.

"Paul Rogers was alive when Ballantyne parted with him. I think the others may have been, too. He pleaded with Paul not to leave him—said he couldn't go back alone."

A pale tongue flickered over pale old lips. "He made a landing, then. We knew he must have when we found the transuranic elements in his body. Go on, go on!"

"The sound of the drill they were using on the door was what roused Ballantyne, I think. It made him remember other sounds. He spoke about the voyage out—it must have been hell. And then . . ."

Comyn's flesh began to quiver as he remembered Ballantyne's voice, his face and the look that had been on it. "Something or someone was calling to Paul, and Ballantyne was begging him not to listen."

Jonas asked harshly, "Who? What?"

"Something he called the Transuranae. He was afraid of them. I think the others had gone to them, and now Paul was going too. He was afraid of them. He screamed."

"And that was all," said Jonas. His eyes were curiously filmed now, like windows curtained lest too much show through. "He was screaming when he died."

Comyn's voice was quite natural when he said, "Oh, no. That wasn't all."

Silence. He waited. Jonas waited. Too much silence. Comyn thought his own heart was pounding as loud as a kettledrum. He was sure all those straining Cochrane ears heard it and knew he was lying. Suddenly he hated them with a personal hatred. They were too big, too strong, too sure of themselves. They wanted too much. Even if knowledge had come to him at that moment that Paul Rogers and all the others were dead and beyond help, he would have gone on fighting the Cochranes, just to mess up their plans. They were too good at using other men for pushballs.

And one of them, he was very sure, had tried to kill him.

Still Jonas waited.

Comyn smiled. "I'll tell the rest of it," he said, "when I'm out by Barnard's Star."

Stanley exploded. "Bluff. Just brazen, stupid bluff. Tell him to go to hell."

Uncle George was talking angrily, and Peter tried to get a word in, but the old man in the chair quieted them with three words.

"Wait a minute." His eyes hadn't left Comyn's. "Wait a minute. There's this to think of. If he isn't bluffing, he could be valuable out there. If he *is*—even so, it might be best to take him along."

They thought that over. They seemed to like it, all but

Stanley. Comyn hadn't had to think; he'd got the meaning of it first.

He looked at Jonas and he said softly, "You *are* a tough old so-and-so, aren't you?"

Jonas chuckled. "Do you want to go to Barnard's Star or don't you?"

Comyn said, between his teeth, "All right, I'll buy it."

"You won't," said Jonas, "be going back to Earth." He looked around at the faces. "That goes for all of you but George. Everything's got to be done right here at Luna, and I'll have no babbling it out till we have a second ship on the way."

Stanley protested, "But what about the courts? United and Trans-World are already entering anti-monopoly suits to get rights to the drive. If they get us tied up—"

"They won't," said Jonas. "George and our legal staff can hold them off. Peter, you get things started here. You're in charge." The old man closed his eyes wearily. "Now get out of here, all of you. I'm tired."

Comyn found himself with the others out in the big hall. They were dismissed, he thought savagely, like a lot of school children.

But the others paid him no attention. They were talking in high voices, Stanley still protesting, Aunt Sally complaining shrilly, until Peter Cochrane's authoritative voice cut across the gabble.

"We'd better get started. Since the work has to be done here, we'll need complete machine-shop facilities and technical staffs. Nielsen and Felder can handle that. You get them here, Bill."

"But to put Ballantyne's drive into a new ship just can't be done here—" Stanley started.

Peter cut him off. "It has to be. One of our new *Pallas* class, I'd say. The locks here will take it. Come on, we'll get things rolling."

Comyn turned and walked away from the noisy, argumentative group. He didn't turn when he heard Sydna calling after him. Right now he'd had enough of the Cochranes. Mixing with the Cochranes had got him into something dandy, something so big that it scared him right down to his boots. And he was in it now, all the way.

The corridor was high and empty, and his footsteps mocked him as he walked. He could walk as far as he pleased—through the rooms and halls, across the terraces, around the gardens blooming in the windless air—but he'd still be under this glass bubble on the Moon. And death was under it with him. Whoever had tried before would try again now, with effort doubled and redoubled, to make sure that one Arch Comyn with his big mouth never lived to peer at Barnard's Star.

And if he did live to get there, and they asked him, Where did Ballantyne land?—what was he going to answer?

That, he didn't know.

VII

COMYN had about reached the limit of his endurance by the time the lid finally blew off everything.

He was in the gardens with Sydna, under a flowering tree that shadowed them from the green Earthlight, when the discreet cough of a servant interrupted.

"Mr. Peter would like to see you at once, miss."

"Is he angry?" asked Sydna.

"I'm afraid so, miss. A message came from the yacht . . ."

"I thought so," she said. And when the servant was gone she added, "Well, let him be mad. It was getting too dull here, all these weeks."

"A nice compliment for me," Comyn remarked.

"Oh, Comyn, I didn't mean us. That's been wonderful."

"Yeah," he said. "And especially wonderful, the way you've let Stanley see us. I appreciate your using me to needle him."

He thought she would hit him, but instead, after a moment, she laughed.

"He is crazy about you, isn't he?" he demanded.

"He's a louse."

"Because he's crazy about you?"

"Because he says so. At least, he did once—just once. Cousin Claudia is a mess, but she is my cousin and she thinks he's wonderful." She straightened down her white dress. "Look at that, you big ape, you've torn the zipper! And anyway, he's one of those earnest asses that bore me stiff. So I *have* let him catch us necking a few times." She spoke suddenly with a bitter undertone. "And anyway, Comyn, between us it's just today. There may not be any tomorrow. When that ship takes off with you inside it—that's it. Shall we go face Peter?"

"What have you done now?"

"You'll find out. I told you, it was getting too dull here."

That, Comyn thought grimly as he followed her, was a

misstatement. It hadn't been dull here under the dome all these weeks, at least not for him. But it had been wearing—very wearing indeed.

The devil of it was that he had had no part whatever in all the feverish, sweating activity that had been going on here. All that work had taken place in the segment of the dome that was completely hidden from the big house by the lines of trees that delimited the gardens.

There were the huge locks where freighters came with loads of fuel for the greedy pumps and furnaces, with chemicals for the air-purifiers and refrigerants for the daytime cooling system, with water for the vast rock cisterns and tanks of oxygen, with food and liquor and supplies. There were the machine shops that had suddenly and swiftly enlarged so that now a small army of expert mechanics labored in them.

There was where the Ballantyne drive was, and the new ship in which it had been installed. It was a larger, stronger and better ship than Ballantyne's—not a pioneer ship but the follow-up to a pioneer, the consolidator. The guts had been stripped out of it and had been put back in a different pattern. The shops rang with a deafening clangor. Men worked in them right up to the limit of efficiency and then were replaced by another shift. Nobody complained. Wages were astronomical. The men were prisoners here until after take-off, but they didn't complain of that, either.

But they, and Peter Cochrane and Simon and Stanley, were part of something, doing something. Even Uncle George, back on Earth using high-priced legal talent to stave off the anti-monopoly suits, was doing something. Only he, Comyn, was barred out.

The armed guards who were stationed beyond the gardens had their orders. A lot of people were posted out, and Comyn was one of them. He could stand and watch the distant silver sides of the ship, and the cranes and the atomic welders flaring, could listen to the booming and screeching and hissing—but that was all.

"Listen," he told Peter Cochrane, "I'm a work-boss and a damned good one. And after all, I'm going in that ship."

"Yes," said Peter, "and you get in it when we go. Not

before then. We've had proof of your capacities for making trouble, Comyn."

"But I could do something outside the ship. I could—"

"No, Comyn. You stay out, and that's final. Grandfather's orders."

Comyn had stayed out, savagely cursing the old man who remained huddled and unseen in his ridiculous room, plotting to steal a star before he died.

He had watched from outside when the ship went out on its first test, slipping silently up into the stark lunar sky. He felt a cold qualm in the belly when he realized that presently he would be inside that same ship, inside a tiny, tiny capsule that held all the light and air and life there was out in the black immensities between the suns.

He had had to wait and watch and sweat, until the ship slipped back and Peter Cochrane came out of it. His face was beaded with sweat and drawn with impatience and something else. Stanley walked jerkily behind him.

". . . whole robot-shift for the drive had bugs in it. The relays won't take the load. Rip it out and rebuild it . . ."

That was all Comyn could find out, just what he overheard. And he was supposed to sit and wait and play games with Sydna and be patient, and he was about ready to blow his fuses one way or another.

Only it seemed that Sydna had blown hers first. He followed her up to the house, and he was sure from the stubborn set of her chin that she was heading into a storm.

Peter was waiting for her on the terrace. He wore the blackest look Comyn had ever seen on a man's face. Stanley and Claudia were there too, as well as a brace of young cousins who looked brightly expectant.

Peter said flatly, "The yacht's due to land in twenty minutes. Captain Moore radioed for clearance, because he's worried. It seems, Sydna, that there are some twenty-odd of your friends aboard."

She said brightly, "Oh, I forgot to tell you about that. I thought a party would liven things up around this detention home."

Peter let go. "You know what we're trying to do here!

You know how much a lot of people would give to know what we're doing! Yet you—"

"Don't be so stuffy, Pete! None of my friends are spies— they don't have brains enough. And anyway they don't care."

"Sure, laugh it off," he said furiously. "Listen, what do you think would happen if word got out that we have a second star-ship almost ready to go? They'd slap an injunction on us in an hour! The only thing that's saved us so far is the fact they don't suspect how fast we're moving. Damn it, Sydna—"

"Stop swearing at me and cool down. Your guards will keep them out of the work-locks. Nobody'll go there anyway if the liquor's here at the house."

"A party would be nice," said Claudia timidly. Then she looked at Stanley and shut up.

Stanley said, "Tell the yacht to go back to Earth." He had aged a good bit since Comyn had first seen him. He had lost that pink, well-fed look, and there was a taut intensity about him that almost matched Peter's. He, too, was going on the second Big Jump. He had insisted on it, and Sally Cochrane had backed him, averring that somebody had to look after her and Claudia's interests. But he didn't seem to enjoy the prospect.

"It can't go back," Sydna said. "People would *know* something was up here if you sent them all back now."

She had them licked, and they knew it. Peter snarled, "All right, Sydna. But if anything goes wrong, I swear I'll break your neck."

Nothing went wrong—not at first. The yacht landed, and from a distance Comyn saw a crowd of gay, squealing young fools pour out of it and make for the house and Sydna and the liquor. And it seemed that almost at once the Earthlit gardens and terraces were full of laughter and dance music and white-jacketed men carrying trays of drinks.

Comyn sat on a terrace and had a few, and a few more, and listened to people having fun. He wasn't having any, not at all. He wasn't sober, but he couldn't let go any more. He knew why too. It was because he wasn't quite one of normal humankind any more, because the shadow of the coming Big Jump was on him, because presently he was going away from it all, out where only five men had ever been before, toward something that could rob you even of a decent death . . .

He wondered, for the thousandth time, what Ballantyne had meant by *the Transuranae*. How could you guess what a thing was when there wasn't any frame of reference at all to go on? They had talked about the Transuranae, but nobody had really had anything to say that could help. The Transuranae—whoever, whatever they were—was it they who had done the thing to Ballantyne that . . .?

Comyn shivered and poured down a little more of the Cochranes' good whisky to drown out the sight and sound of Ballantyne, dead and stirring in his high-barred bed. All of a sudden a pretty girl with dark fluffy hair was standing in front of him, asking: "Who are you?"

She was cute as a button. She made him feel old, and suddenly there was an uncrossable gulf between them because of the thing he was going to do and that she was not going to do and didn't even know about. But she was cute.

"I don't know," he said. "I'm a stranger here, myself. Who are you?"

"You'll never guess."

"Then I won't try."

"I'm Bridget," she said, and made a face. "Awful name, isn't it?" All at once she brightened, looking over Comyn's head. "Oh, there's Simon!" She called his name and waved, and Simon came over and put his arm around her and she sort of melted in against him, smiling, but still interested in Comyn.

"Simon, he's unhappy. Why is he unhappy?"

"He thinks people are trying to kill him. Has anybody tried it lately, Comyn?"

"I haven't turned my back on anybody," Comyn said.

"You're joking," said Bridget. "Nobody would want to kill him—he's cute."

"Well," said Simon, "that's a word I wouldn't have thought of to describe him, but maybe you're right. Come on, Bridgie. So long, Comyn, and don't take any poisoned Martinis."

Comyn watched them go. His lack of affection for Simon

Cochrane was reaching gigantic proportions. He was thinking how nice it was going to be for all of them, cooped up together in a ship all the way out to Barnard's Star.

He saw Peter come out on the terrace and stand scowling at the festivities. He was stone-cold sober. Stanley joined him, and he wasn't having any fun either. They talked a minute or two, and then Peter went down into the garden and vanished into the darkness. Going to check on his cordon of guards, Comyn thought. Sydna ought to get a good licking for this. But then, it was just such a trick of Sydna's that had got him here, so he ought to be grateful—or ought he?

Where was Sydna, anyway?

Stanley went down the steps and into the garden, after Peter. Comyn got up. He was tired of sitting and brooding. He searched around for a sight of Sydna's blonde head, spotted it and went toward it. The terrace felt a bit unsteady under his feet, and there seemed to be two or three hundred people on it instead of only some twenty-odd. Sydna was with the long drink of water she called Johnny, the one Comyn had met before. There were several others around them. Somebody had just said something very funny, and they were all laughing.

Comyn came up beside Sydna and said, "Hello."

She looked up at him. Her eyes were very bright, very gay. "Hello, Comyn." On the other side of her, Johnny stood up.

Comyn said, "How about entertaining a visiting fireman?"

She shook her head. "You look glum. I don't feel like being glum." She turned away.

Comyn put his hand on her shoulder. "Sydna . . ."

"Oh, go away, Comyn. I'm enjoying myself. Let me alone."

Johnny stepped between them. He was feeling good. He was feeling strong and twice his normal size. He thrust his face into Comyn's and said, "You heard her. Go away."

Comyn's temper, none too long at the best, ran out with a snap. He picked Johnny up and set him aside. "Listen, Sydna, I want to talk to you . . ."

Johnny's fist hit him on the cheekbone, hard enough to make his head ring.

"Now will you go?" asked Johnny. His breath was coming hard and excited, and he was all ready to let go again. Sydna sprang to her feet, slamming her glass down on the low table in front of her.

"Oh, the devil with both of you!" she snapped, and strode away, taking the others with her. Comyn glowered after her, thinking that some day he would beat that arrogance out of her if he kept his health.

Johnny said, "I think we better go out in the garden."

Comyn looked at him. "Oh, no!"

Johnny's face was pale, except for two red bars along his cheekbones. He had worked himself up to a fine pitch, and he wasn't going to let it go. "You've been trying to take Sydna away from me," he said.

Comyn laughed.

The red bars widened on Johnny's face until they reached from his collar to the roots of his hair.

"You come into the garden," he said, "or I'll do it right here."

He would too. Comyn sighed. "Okay, Junior, come on. Maybe I can talk some sense into you out there."

They went down the steps, close together. There was a rustling and cooing as of pigeons in the dark fringe of shrubbery, and Comyn led on. Johnny tramped beside him, his breath whistling in his nose. Comyn grinned. Johnny sounded like a very young and angry bull at courting time.

The lights of the terrace dimmed and passed away behind them, and the stars grew very bright, burning against the dome. The voices were only a distant murmur.

Johnny said, "This is far enough."

"Okay." Comyn stopped. "Hold on a minute, kid, and listen—"

He ducked, and Johnny's arm swung violently past his head. Then the kid was all over him. Comyn smacked him open-handed a couple of times, impatiently, but the kid was full of himself. He was strong enough, and some of his blows hurt. Comyn began to get mad.

"Lay off," he said, "or I'll give it to you, kid or no kid."

He pushed him away. Johnny muttered something about Comyn being scared to fight. Suddenly he rushed him. Comyn sidestepped.

From out of the dense shadows of a stand of tall white-flowering bushes came a narrow bolt of lightning. It struck, with a crack and a flare, on the spot which Comyn had just left and which Johnny was just now passing. The kid went down without a whimper.

Comyn stood for one dazed instant looking from the dead boy to the dark mass of bushes. Then he moved, faster than he had ever moved before. A second bolt from a shocker turned up to lethal voltage hit the ground behind him. It knocked him over, half stunned, but that was all, and he never stopped going, rolling in among a clump of trees. He got his own weapon into his hand. He pushed the stud all the way up and fired into the bushes, but a little high. He wanted to flush the killer out, alive.

Sounds began to come from the direction of the house. They had seen the man-made lightning playing. Some woman screamed, and men were shouting. Comyn fired twice more into the bushes, changing his position fast each time. The killer didn't answer, and then beyond the bushes he heard somebody running. Comyn went after him.

People were pouring out into the gardens from the house now. The killer couldn't turn that way. He could try to double back toward the passenger lock, but Comyn would be in his way and Comyn was armed. Maybe the killer hadn't counted on this. He went the only way there was left open, toward the freight locks. Comyn ran, turning down the power on his shocker. It didn't carry far that way, but if he could get close enough he might bring down the guy alive and still able to talk.

He saw him, running fast across an open glade. He shouted to him to stop, but he was outranged. The only answer he got was a snap bolt that hit a tree too close for comfort. There were shouts and thrashings in the gardens all around now, and the emergency lights were coming on. The guards were moving in from the freight locks. The killer ran, but there was no place to run to. And then there were men on all sides of him in the bright glare of the lights, and the blue bolts flashed and struck . . . and that was it.

Comyn came up. There was a milling around of people. Guards were shoving the workmen back into the lock and there was a lot of talking. Peter Cochrane and Stanley were both there, both with shockers in their hands, looking at the body. Comyn looked too.

"Do you know him?" he asked.

Peter nodded, and Stanley said, "Name's Washburn. He used to be a Cochrane employee—oh, two, three years ago. He was fired. Undesirable, a trouble-maker." Stanley shook his head. "How did he get here? What was he doing?"

Comyn said, "Trying to kill me. He tried it once before, on Earth."

Peter looked at him sharply. "You're sure of that?"

Comyn nodded.

People were coming from the party now! Sydna, Simon, guests looking excited, frightened, upset, or curious, according to their natures.

"Keep them back," said Peter savagely. "Keep them away from here."

Comyn said, "It doesn't matter now. You might as well let them see the ship. It doesn't matter."

Peter stared at him. Simon moved between them, looking down. "Hey," he said. "Hey, he came aboard the yacht. I saw him."

Peter's eyes blazed. "And you didn't stop him? You let a character like that come in here and didn't even tell me?"

Simon said angrily, "Are you kidding? He had a pass from you."

Without a word, Comyn turned and took Peter Cochrane by the neck and bore him down.

Hands pulled at him. There was a confusion of voices. Finally somebody hit him across the back of the head with the flat of a shocker. He let go and they dragged him away off of Peter. Peter got up unsteadily. Stanley was down on his knees beside the dead man, going through his pockets. He held up a piece of paper.

"Here it is, Peter. It has your signature."

Peter shook his head. He took the paper and studied it.

"Forgery," he said. "He worked for us. He could have got hold of a signature very easily. Probably on his termination-of-contract papers. I've signed a lot of 'em. I never gave him a pass."

Comyn said, "I hope you can prove that." Men were still holding his arms, and his head hurt. Peter Cochrane came up to him.

"Why? And what did you mean by, 'Let them see the ship. It doesn't matter now'?"

Comyn said slowly, "Your friend was in too much of a hurry. He thought he had a clear shot at me, but he didn't. Johnny got in the way."

A silence fell. It spread outward from Comyn, stunned and heavy, and in it Sydna's voice was harsh and very loud.

"You mean Johnny's dead."

"Dead. You can bury Washburn and you could have buried me, but you can't bury Johnny. And I'm glad. He was a fool kid, but this wasn't any of his fight. There was no reason he should die for it."

He looked around at them, at Peter and Simon and Bill Stanley and at Sydna with her shocked white face—particularly at Sydna.

"Well, you had your party," he said bitterly. "And it's blown the lid right off your private country on the Moon. You'll have Earth policemen tramping all over it, and you can't keep them out. They'll want to know all about how Johnny got killed, and why, and what you're doing here that's worth a murder, and there won't be any secret about it anywhere. That's why I say you might as well let them know about the ship."

Again there was a long, cold silence. The dead man lay on his side where Stanley had rolled him. One arm flung carelessly across his face. His mouth seemed to be smiling, as if he were dreaming. Stanley looked gray and sick, and Simon's eyes roved uneasily, not looking at anything. Behind the people the freight locks towered upward, and out from them came the muffled clang and roar that had not stopped even for death.

Peter Cochrane spoke.

"I will notify the Earth authorities myself. Meanwhile,

no one is to leave the dome or communicate with anyone until the investigation is complete and the police allow you to go."

There was a loud cry of protest. Peter silenced it.

"I'm sorry, it's necessary. You are welcome as our guests, and I'm sure Sydna will make your visit as pleasant as possible."

They began to straggle away slowly, back toward the house. Some men went to hunt for Johnny. Peter turned again to Comyn.

"I haven't tried to kill you. As Jonas told you, murder is for fools. And if I had wanted to kill you I'd have done it myself and it wouldn't have been bungled. All right, boys, let him go."

Then Peter Cochrane went off, walking fast, toward the freight locks. Simon watched him go uneasily.

"You know what he'll do," he said to Stanley.

Stanley was still staring at the body. It seemed to have a strange fascination for him. He ran his tongue constantly over his lips as though they were dry, and his hands shook.

"I don't know," he answered absently. "I haven't had time to think."

"He'll hold off notifying Earth as long as he can. He'll get the bloody ship ready for take-off and go, without any further tests. By the time the cops get here, we'll be clear out of the System—if the drive works."

His voice lingered over the brief word, *if*. Comyn heard him and shivered, wondering where they would be if it didn't.

VIII

HIS NAME WAS Arch Comyn, and once he had had a home on Earth, and once he had had a girl with strong brown shoulders. *And what was he doing out here in the abyss between the stars?*

From across the main cabin, from the table where some of the others were playing cards, a voice said:

"Give me three."

Comyn thought it was funny. It was very funny, indeed, that men making the second Big Jump in history, that men going faster and farther than any men but five had ever gone before, separated only by metal walls from the awfulness of infinity, should sit and play games with little plastic cards and pretend that they were not where they were.

He knew now what Ballantyne had felt. This was not the going between worlds that men had grown used to. This was an adventure into madness. The ports were shielded tight because there was nothing beyond them but an awful blankness, tinged with eerie flickerings of energy that was their own mass discharging itself through the neutronic convertors into a tight propulsion field, hurling them through a space that was not normal and might not even exist in their own universe. Theoretically, the astrogators knew where they were. Actually, no one knew.

The nastiest thing about it was that there was no sense of motion. The interior of the ship was gripped in a stasis that was the reactionless core of the mass-propulsion field itself, the dead quiet eye of the hurricane. They might as well have been in a tightly shuttered room on Earth, going nowhere. And yet the stars—the stars that Ballantyne had learned to hate—showed on the screens as crawling tracks, distorted and spectral and infinitely strange, as the unthinkably speeding ship overtook and passed their light rays.

Only one screen, fitted with a complicated electronic damper-field, showed space ahead in relatively true perspective. Centered in the cross-hairs and kept centered by automatic compensators was the dull red eye of Barnard's Star. At first, the men had stared often at the screen and the brooding eye in it. Then they had looked at it less and less, and finally avoided it altogether.

Comyn couldn't avoid it. He'd gone back to stare at it again and again. He couldn't stop thinking about it. He asked Peter Cochrane now, "Why Barnard's Star, anyway? What made Ballantyne pick it instead of Centauri?"

"We know Barnard's Star has planets," said Peter. He looked worn, drawn to the breaking point, full of a feverish triumph that would not let him rest. "It has a low luminosity, and the astronomers were able to separate its planets visually some years ago, with the Keble telescope. Alpha and Proxima Centauri they're still not sure of, so Barnard was chosen. Of course, it's only a start. The Weiszacker theory is pretty well proved by now, and it postulates that most stars have planets, so you can see this is only a start—"

He broke off suddenly, as though he realized he was talking too rapidly, too intensely. The young doctor who had cared for Ballantyne and who was going to take care of them now because he was the only expert there was on transuranic medicine, said:

"Better take a sedative and knock off for a while, Mr. Cochrane."

Peter said, "No, I want to go over these log books again."

"There's plenty of time for log books."

"There's nothing in them we haven't already found out, anyway," Simon said. His gaze, cold and glowering, was fixed on Comyn. "Our friend here is the only one who knows where we're going. Or does he?"

"You'll find out," said Comyn, "when we get there."

French, the doctor, and Roth, the physicist who had examined Ballantyne, and the other men from the Cochrane labs who were playing cards, bent studiously over their game to keep out of Cochrane quarrels.

Comyn said harshly to Peter, Simon and Bill Stanley, "And before you find out, I'm going to know which of you hired Washburn to do me in."

"Which one of us?"

"Yes. It was one of you three. One of you has the missing books of Ballantyne's log. You all had the opportunity."

Comyn's eyes were very bright, very hard. He was, like the rest of them, suffering from long tension. Things had been bad before they left Luna: Johnny's sheeted corpse lying in one of the great rooms; Sydna's guests hysterically demanding to know why the police didn't come, why they were being kept prisoner—and Sydna herself, with a face like a stone image, not speaking to anyone. Old Jonas had talked to her. What he had said, Comyn didn't know, but Sydna had no spirit left in her.

It hadn't really gone on long. No more than two days, Earth time. Peter had done exactly as Simon predicted. The activity around the freight locks had reached an insane pitch, with workmen dropping in their tracks and being revived or replaced. And then, incredibly, the ship was ready, Peter called the authorities, and there was not even time to say good-bye.

"One of you," Comyn said, "hired that killer who got the wrong man. I'm not sure yet which one of you it was. But I will be."

Peter said furiously, "You still think I gave Washburn that pass?"

"He had it."

Simon came and stood in front of Comyn. "I didn't like you the first time I saw you," he said. "I like you less and less as time goes by. You talk too much. It might be a good idea if someone did kill you."

"Yeah," said Comyn. "And you saw Washburn get off the yacht. You could have stopped him and checked that forged pass, but you didn't."

Bill Stanley caught Simon's arm and said, "Wait a minute. We can't afford any brawls now. We . . ."

Doctor French cleared his throat nervously. "Listen, we're under a psychological strain that can crack us wide open if we're not careful. Knock it off. Take a sedative, calm down. Especially you, Mr. Cochrane."

"You sound," said Peter dryly, "as though you could use a sedative yourself." He glanced at Simon. "However, I think you're right. Let it go, Simon."

"You'd better let it go, too. But I won't argue it now. I'm going to try to sleep."

He went off to his cabin. Simon had disappeared. Bill Stanley sat down by himself and stared blankly at a bulkhead. The card players talked in low monotones, not as though their minds were on the game.

Comyn lit a cigarette and moved restlessly back and forth in the confined space. Air whirred in the ventilators. The dome lights burned, and they were bright enough, but there was something vaguely unnatural about the light itself, as though it had shifted somewhere along the spectrum. Comyn's flesh quivered deep in its individual cells, torturing him like a persistent itch. It tortured everybody. Roth had said it was some obscure effect of the stasis and its surrounding field of energy. Static electricity, he thought, generated by their own bodies under the abnormal conditions. One of the hazards of star-flight. It could be a hazard. Little things could grow so big. Little things like an itch or a sound you couldn't quite hear.

Comyn thought: *Ballantyne heard it at the last. All the way out to Barnard's Star and back he listened to it, but he couldn't hear it. And then they fetched the damned electric drill and that was it—the sound . . .*

Just over the threshold of hearing lay the nerve-aching screech and whine, the incessant, maddening, unbearable sound—the sound of the drive.

Comyn swore abruptly, and said, "It wouldn't be so bad if we were moving."

Roth grunted, scowling at the cards he held. "You're moving," he said. "You're covering six light-years a lot of times faster than light itself." He threw down his hand. "A lousy pair of tens. I'm out. Yes, Comyn, you're moving."

"But how do we know we are? We can't feel it, we can't see it, we can't even hear it."

"We take it on faith," said Roth. "Our instruments assure us that we're approaching Barnard's Star at high velocity. Or it's approaching us. Who knows? Motion is only relative. Anyway, relative to our known universe we're going at a speed that's so fast it's impossible—theoretically. Relative to some other universe or state of matter, we could easily be standing still."

"When you scientists start dreaming it up, you give me a pain," said Comyn. "It all sounds cockeyed."

"Not at all. Groom's theory, on which Ballantyne built his drive, was that the so-called light-speed barrier was real, and that matter achieving faster-than-light velocities would shift into another plane of atomic vibration, or matter-state, creating a closed vacuum in the continuum in which energy could be neither gained nor lost. Hence, the mass-propulsion field, the ship feeding on itself, as it were, using the kinetic energy stored up in the original acceleration. The drive works, but whether or not that proves the theory, we don't know. There's a very interesting distortion of time . . ."

Comyn, listening and only half understanding, felt that nightmare sense of unreality closer upon him. He fought against it; he had to keep his mind on the very real and nasty problem that faced Arch Comyn.

". . . and Vickrey was much concerned with time in his notes on the outward voyage," Roth was saying. "The chronometers functioned, but were they still accurate as to Earth chronology? There was no way to check. We say they took so-and-so many months for the first Big Jump. Vickrey's word was 'eternity'—a fairly vague term. How long has it been since we went into star-drive? My idea is that the time-sense . . ."

Comyn stamped out his cigarette irritably and left the main cabin. All this scientific double-talk was upsetting. He had a literal mind. A chair was a chair, a table was a table and an hour was sixty minutes long. As long as he could hang onto these realities, he could make out.

He dug a bottle out of a locker—not the sedative Doctor French would have prescribed, but ninety-proof and good enough. He sat drinking it and thinking of Sydna, wondering if she really meant what she had said about there not being any tomorrow for them. Probably. He wished she was here, but he was glad she wasn't. After a while he began to listen to the drive: the sound he could hear with the edges of his teeth and the raw ends of his nerves, but not quite with his ears. He swore, poured another drink and then went to sleep. It seemed a devil of a way to spend your time on this, man's second traverse between the stars, but there wasn't much else to do. Even the scientists had little to do but check their instruments. The flight engineers were useful only when shifting in or out of drive, and the pilots were purely ornamental except when the ship was operating on normal velocity. The functioning of the ship on star-drive was automatic. No crew of human beings could have controlled it manually. All they did was sit and watch a million gadgets and hope they worked.

Comyn snored, twitched and dreamed. His dreams were not good. He started up, gagging on a lungful of stale air— it seemed to him that he hadn't breathed real air since he went to Luna—and became aware of the bell that announced mealtime.

Comyn came out of his cabin warily, as he always did. He was not afraid of guns. The ship's arsenal was locked, and no one was allowed anything more lethal than a pocket-knife. Peter Cochrane was taking no chances with hysteria, space fever or simple mutiny. But a man bent on murder can be very ingenious in devising weapons. Comyn was cautious.

There was no one in the corridor. Comyn yawned and started along it toward the main cabin. His head was still heavy, and there was a strong taste of whisky in his mouth.

On the starboard side of the corridor was a compartment used for the keeping of certain stores for the cabin section. The door was not quite shut, but that was not unusual since people went in and out of it fairly often. Comyn passed it.

There was a swift, sharp suction of air behind him, a door being pulled open silently but very fast, and then a hurried step and one harsh indrawn breath. Comyn threw himself forward and as much to the left as he could manage on split-second notice. The steel bar that had been meant for the back of his skull came whistling down onto his right shoulder instead. It made a very ugly noise.

Pain became a huge inescapable fact. He was falling and he couldn't help that, but his left hand went instinctively to the focal point of that agony as though to hold it back, and found instead the collared end of the steel bar and gripped it and pulled it along.

He hit the deck. Bands of light were flickering in front of his eyes, and there was darkness close behind. But the fear of death was on him and he thrashed around, still holding the steel bar. There was a man there, a cautious man, a man expecting failure, because he had hidden his face and head so that his victim could not recognize him— all this care despite the fact that there should have been no possibility of recognition.

Rage came up in Comyn so strongly that it almost cleared away that gathering dark. He made an animal sound, with no words in it, and tried to get up. The man with the hidden face turned suddenly and ran away. His legs and his polished shoes ran and ran down the length of the passage, and Comyn watched them, and he knew whose shoes they were, and he recognized those dark-trousered legs. A man's face is only part of what you know him by. He started to say the name that went with them, but he didn't have time. He passed out.

He was still lying in the corridor. His right arm was numb to the finger ends, and he felt pain when he moved. It took him a long time to get up, and a longer time to make the several miles down the passage and into the main cabin. He had not been out too long. They were still at dinner, around the collapsible tables. The men looked at him when he came in. There were all there, Peter and Simon and Bill Stanley, the scientists, all of them. They stopped eating and Doctor French got up suddenly.

Comyn sat down heavily. He looked at Peter Cochrane. "I'm ready now," he said, "to tell you where Ballantyne landed."

IX

MANY VOICES spoke at once. French was bending over him, asking where he was hurt. Peter Cochrane stood up, demanding silence. Simon was leaning forward, his eyes intent. Bill Stanley put down his knife and fork. His hands were seized with an uncontrollable trembling. There was a pallor on him and a sweating. Comyn laughed.

"You should have made it good," he said to William Stanley. "Peter would have. Simon would have. But not you. You haven't that kind of guts."

Stanley said, "I don't—"

"Oh, yes, you do. Hiding your face didn't hide the rest of you. I know your shoes, your clothes, the way you move. I know you, now."

Stanley pushed his chair back a little, as though he would like to get away from Comyn, from all of them. He spoke again, but his words were not clear.

"It's different when you have to do it yourself, isn't it?" Comyn said. "Not nice and tidy like just writing a check. You have to figure on maybe missing the first time. You have to be able to go on hitting a man until he stays down. You have to have a strong stomach and no nerves, like Washburn. Maybe with a gun you could have done it, but not with your hands—not ever with your hands."

French was trying to peel his shirt back, and Comyn pushed him away. Simon had risen. His eyes met Peter's. Peter's face got white around the lips. Suddenly he took hold of Stanley's jacket.

"Did you do this, Bill?"

Stanley sat perfectly still, looking up at Peter. His eyes began to get a slow hot gleam in them that grew brighter and uglier, and then all at once he struck Peter's hand away and sprang up. It seemed as though that rough touch on him had acted as a key to turn loose everything that had been bottled up in him under pressure for a long time.

It came out quietly, very quietly, as though his throat was pulled too tight to make much noise in it.

"Yes, I did. And keep your hands off me."

He moved back a step or two, away from them. Nobody spoke around the tables. They were all watching, with their forks halfway to their mouths. Simon started forward, but Peter caught him.

"That won't do any good right now," he said. And then to Stanley: "You have the log books."

"I had them. I burned them." He looked from Peter to Simon and back again. "Getting them was easy. You were all so excited, thinking what you might be going to get. There were only two of them—thin little books. I saw them first and stuck them inside my shirt, as easy as that."

"You burned them," Peter said, and Stanley jerked his head.

"I memorized them. I have a good memory." He turned on Comyn. "All right, go ahead. Tell them. You've made trouble for me from the beginning. I'd have had you killed on Mars, only Peter stopped it."

Comyn said, "Doesn't Johnny weigh a little heavy on your soul?"

"No. That was Washburn's doing. I didn't even know he was there until I saw him dead. I fired him after he failed the first time. You cost him a lot of money, Comyn, and he was mad. I guess he thought he could still collect. Probably blackmail me too. No, Johnny wasn't my fault."

"I don't understand, Bill," said Peter. He was staring at Stanley in a puzzled way, shaking his head slowly from side to side. "Why? We always treated you right. You were one of the family, you had an important job, plenty of money—we trusted you. I don't understand."

Stanley laughed. It was not a nice sound. "One of the family," he repeated. "An appendage. A wailing wall for Claudia, and a football for her mother. A convenience. Good old dependable Bill. But not a Cochrane, never for a minute. No real voice in anything, no real interest in the corporation. That was all Claudia's." His mouth twisted. "Claudia!"

Simon said angrily, "What did you marry her for, then? You were anxious enough at the time."

"What would anybody marry Claudia for?" asked Stanley. "Her money. I thought I could stick it out, but between her and her old bat of a mother—" He broke off. "All right. I saw a chance to get hold of something worth having and I took it. What's wrong with that? Ask old Jonas how many times he did it, to get his palace on the Moon."

Comyn repeated his original statement about himself. "You should have made it good."

"I should have. Unfortunately, I don't have the capacity for violence. Few civilized men do." His control was beginning to crack a little. He had started to shake again, and his eyes blazed. Comyn thought how unfamiliar a man looked with all his emotions showing. It was like seeing him with his clothes off.

Stanley turned again to Peter and the smouldering Simon. His voice had risen just a little, a notch higher, a notch louder. "Comyn says he can tell you where Ballantyne landed. All right. But I read the log, remember. I know the coordinates, not just the world but the exact location on it. I know where the transuranic ores are, the exact location. I know—"

Peter said, "I think we could find them if we had to."

"Perhaps you could. But there's more than just finding them. There's the—the Transuranae. I know about them too." He strode toward Comyn, four or five jerky steps. "Do you know all that, Comyn? Can you tell them?"

Comyn didn't answer for a long moment. Then he said slowly, "Stanley, you're a scared little man, a greedy little man, and you're hoping against hope. But you're safe. You win." He glanced at Peter. "I thought maybe I could jar it out of him, but it didn't work. I can't tell you where Ballantyne landed. I never knew."

Peter let out a long breath. "I hoped," he said, "but I never counted on it. So that settles that." He looked at Stanley. "Well?"

Stanley was trying hard to hang onto himself. The sudden uncontested victory had almost unmanned him. He tried three times before he could get the words out.

"Let's not be polite about this. For once, I've got the upper hand and there's nothing you can do about it. You can't even kill me, because all the knowledge is in my head and because you're going to need me every step of the way, before we land and after. Especially after."

"Suppose," said Peter softly, "that we decide we don't need you at all. Suppose we just lock you up and let you stay there."

"You could. It would be dangerous and tremendously expensive to search eight unknown planets—there are satellites too, you know. Our fuel and supplies aren't unlimited. The voyage alone was Ballantyne's whole objective, and the landing was only by the way. But we're here to consolidate, and we can't waste too much potential running around. You could try, and you might even succeed. But without the information I can give you, you'd never get the ores. You probably would not even survive the attempt. There are . . . obstacles."

The shadow of dread that passed over Stanley's face was more impressive than any threat, because it was personal and unpremeditated. And Comyn was remembering Ballantyne's final scream.

"What's your price?" asked Peter Cochrane.

"High," said Stanley, "but not too high. I want a controlling interest in Cochrane Transuranic and all that goes with it. Fifty-one percent. You Cochranes have enough, Peter. There's no reason why you should have this too."

For a while nobody spoke. There were deep lines between Peter's eyes and around his mouth. Simon watched Stanley with the cold eagerness of a leopard. Finally Peter said:

"What do you think, Simon?"

"Tell him where to go. The Cochranes have never needed help from little swine like him."

Again no one spoke. Peter scowled and thought. Sweat gathered in drops on Stanley's forehead and ran slowly down his temples, over pulses that were beating visibly.

Peter said thoughtfully, "We might beat it out of him." His gaze slid to Comyn. "What do you think?"

"I'd enjoy it," Comyn said. "But it's risky business. None of us are experts, and you can kill a man without meaning to. Besides, in this case it wouldn't work. All Stanley has to do is break down and tell us a bunch of lies, and we wouldn't know the difference. We couldn't check it." He paused, and added, "I think he's got you."

Simon started a bitter protest, and Peter silenced him. "It comes down to this," he said. "A hundred percent or forty-nine. It won't make any difference if we come back the way Ballantyne did. Very well, Bill, you win."

"I want it on paper," Stanley said. "And signed."

"You'll get it. And now I'm going to tell you what I think of you." He told him, and Stanley listened. When he was all through, Stanley said:

"You were entitled to that, but I don't want any more of it, from either of you. Do you understand?"

He seemed to have grown several inches taller, and his face had acquired a superficial calm that was almost dignified. He started to leave the cabin, a proud man, a successful man, and then Comyn said quietly:

"Do you think this is going to make Sydna fall at your feet?"

Stanley turned around. He said, "I don't know why I didn't beat your head in when I had the chance. You keep your dirty mouth shut."

"What is this," demanded Peter, "about Sydna?"

Comyn said, "He'd rather have her than Claudia."

Simon laughed. He seemed to find that idea so genuinely funny that he couldn't help laughing. Stanley rounded on him in a white fury.

"Sydna's standards aren't so high. Ask Comyn. And you're going to learn something, all of you. You're going to learn to respect me. Sydna too. She has nothing to be haughty about except her money. None of you have. You can all think what you like about me, but by God you'll respect me!"

He gave Simon a crack across the mouth that stopped his laughter, and then he went away so swiftly and furiously that he was gone before Simon could get at him. Peter hauled his brother away toward his own cabin.

"Keep your temper," he said. "We've got enough on our necks. Come on, we have work to do."

They left. The men around the table began slowly to eat again, not as though they cared about it. They didn't talk. They were too embarrassed by what had happened and now waited till they could get off by themselves in small groups to let loose the excited chatter that was in them. French said to Comyn:

"Better let me take care of that shoulder."

He took care of it, and it was not as bad as it might have been because Comyn's muscles were thick and had saved the bone. But he was pretty well laid up with it for a while. By the time he could use his arm again he was ready to lose his mind from inaction, from the subliminal screech of the drive, from the not-moving and not-seeing—the uncanny drawing out of time.

He looked at his watch, and it meant nothing. The chronometers were only a mockery. Earth was years, centuries behind them, and Barnard's Star had grown no bigger on the screen, no brighter. The feeling had begun to grow on the ship's company that they were lost somewhere out of space and time and would never find their way back. There were outbreaks of hysteria, and French was busy with his needle. One man cracked completely and was confined to his cabin, strapped down.

"We'll all be there," muttered French, "if we don't get out of this pretty soon."

"We're almost ready to shift drive," Peter said. His face was pared down to the bone now, and he looked more like Jonas and more like an Indian than ever. "We'll be back in normal space—tomorrow."

He hesitated before he said that word that was only an arbitrary symbol for something that didn't exist.

"If we make it," Comyn thought. The fear was in him too. It was the strangeness that got you, the not knowing. You had to sit and wait and wonder if the trap would let you go.

Stanley kept saying, "Don't worry. Ballantyne and the others felt the way we do, but they came out of it all right. They made it."

He had his paper, signed and sealed. He knew more about what was going to happen than any of them. But even he was afraid. It showed on him like a gray dust, and his cheering words were only words and nothing more. Nobody answered him. People rarely spoke to him any more. Comyn thought that it wasn't their concern over the Cochrane fortunes, but simply that the men hated to have their lives depending on Stanley.

They didn't trust him, not because of his business ethics but because they felt he was not a man, except by courtesy of sex. He was no longer pink and prosperous, but he was still the executive errand-boy, the carrier-out of other men's orders. They had seen the way he had won his victory. It did not inspire confidence in them.

"As soon as we're out of drive," Stanley told Peter, "I'll give you the coordinates on our destination."

The flight engineers were glued to their instruments now. Time passed, or the arbitrary illusion of it, measured off by the chronometers. Men moved about, doing nothing in particular with great intensity, or simply sat and sweated. They had been through this once, and it had been bad enough. This time it was worse. The interior of the ship felt to Comyn like the inside of a bomb getting ready to explode. The red eye of Barnard's Star watched them from the screen and did not change.

The dome lights began to flash off and on. Alarm bells rang through the passageways and in the cabins. The first warning. French finished giving the last man his shot.

"All right," said Peter. "Everybody to your quarters." His voice was rasping, like an old man's. Up in the control room the pilots were strapping in, ready to take over. Indicators quivered and crawled, and a sonic-relay beam was squeaking higher and higher up the scale. Lights flickered on the board like little stars. The engineers were as robots, eyes fixed, faces glazed with sweat, calling off in voices that were not human. The astrogators were standing by.

Somebody said, "What if they miscalculated? What if we ram right into Barnard's Star?"

Comyn went back to his cabin and lay down. He felt sick. He wanted a drink worse than he ever had in his life, but there wasn't any more. He rolled the coppery taste of fear over his tongue and braced himself. The dome lights were still flashing: Off, on; off, on.

The bells rang—second warning.

Comyn waited. The shot was supposed to dull the nerves, make the shock easier on them. His did not feel dulled. He was afraid of what was coming and more afraid of its not coming. Suppose the drive failed to shift? Suppose they couldn't come out of it?

The dome lights flashed, off, on. It was hard on the eyes, hard on the nerves. The squall and screech of the drive was almost audible now. He waited, and it was a long time, too long.

Something had gone wrong; the drive had failed and they couldn't come out of it. They were going to go on and on forever in this not-space until they went crazy and died, and even that wouldn't stop them . . .

The lights stopped flashing. They stayed a hard bright steady glare, and then the third warning sounded, not bells this time but a siren, so there would be no mistake about it. The wild banshee howling raised the hair on Comyn's head and brought out the cold sweat on his skin, and then the lights went out and there was no more sound.

Darkness. The black silence of the tomb. He strained his ears, but even the supersonic torture of the drive was slipping away, receding beyond reach. Blue witch-lights flared from every metal surface in the ship, and then it began: the subtle slide and wrench and twist that took each separate atom in a man's body and moved it in a new direction with the most horrible effect of vertigo that had ever been devised. Comyn tried to scream, but whether he made it or not he never knew. For one timeless ghastly interval he thought he saw the fabric of the ship itself dissolving with him into a mist of discrete particles, and he knew that he wasn't human any more and that nothing was real. And then he plunged headlong into nothingness.

X

THE FIRST thing that came to him was the familiar thud and throb of the auxiliaries. It dragged him back to the point where he could remember what his name was, and then he opened his eyes and sat up. There were solid bulkheads around him, and a solid bunk under him. He felt himself all over, and he was still there. The feel of the ship was different. It was the normal feel of a spaceship, under way and braking.

He got up and went out into the passageway. The lights were on again. Men were coming out of their cabins. He wondered if he looked like them, like something dug up and resurrected. His legs didn't work right and he staggered, trying to run. But they were all staggering and nobody noticed. There was a rising babble of voices. The ship sounded like an aviary at dawn.

He came into the main cabin. He saw faces with tears running down them, but he didn't know whose they were and he didn't care. The ports were open. For the first time in a million years the blank walls were opened up, and Comyn flung himself toward the nearest port. Men crowded on his heels and there was much noise, but he neither felt nor heard. He clung to the thick quartzite and stared at the beautiful deep darkness of space outside. He saw the stars that were no longer eerie crawling worms of light but bright suns, blazing blue and red and gold and green. They hung in clusters, in ropes and chains and burning clouds against the primal night.

Somebody said, in one long tumbling breath: "We made it oh God we made it we shifted back!"

Comyn made himself stop shaking. He looked around the cabin, but the people he wanted were not there and he went forward to the bridge. The brake bursts shook the deck plates under his feet, and it was a good feeling. They were back. They were moving. Everything was all right.

Peter and Simon and Stanley were in the bridge. The ports were open here too, and dead ahead in space was a far-off sun the color of rusty iron—a somber fire burning in the dark. Comyn's feeling of elation drained away. They had made the second Big Jump, and now it was waiting for them under the light of that mad and wildly fleeing star—the world and the fate that had waited for Ballantyne at the end of that first long trail.

Stanley had a sheet of paper, a large one, covered with many figures. He held it out to the navigator.

"Here's your destination," he said.

The navigator spread out the paper on his workboard and scowled at it. Presently he said, "You've given me too much, mister. The planetary coordinates look okay, and the orbital velocity and grav-constant equations and the landing speeds. But all this mess here—these calculations of the relative motions of Ballantyne's ship and Barnard II . . . !"

Comyn reached over and snatched the paper out of the startled man's hands. He backed away, looking at it, ignoring the sudden angry words that were being said.

He said to Stanley, "You memorized all this?"

"Of course," said Stanley. He made a grab for the paper. "Damn you, Comyn."

"Yes, you did," said Comyn, and tore the sheet apart.

An enraged and startled cry burst out from several different throats, and Comyn thrust the torn scraps into his pockets. He smiled at Stanley.

"You can write it out again."

Peter swore, a bitter vitriolic stream. "What are you trying to do, Comyn? Aren't things tough enough without—"

"He memorized it all," said Comyn. "He's good. He can remember stuff in three dimensions, orbital velocities, landing speeds, the works. Give him a pencil and paper. He can write it out again."

A glint of understanding came all at once into Peter's eyes. "Sure," he said. "Get him some paper, Simon. I'm sorry this happened, Bill, but there's nothing lost except a little work."

"A little work," said Stanley. He looked at Comyn the

way a cobra looks at something it can't get at to strike. He said things, very ugly things, but Comyn didn't pay attention to them. He was noticing some sudden changes in Stanley.

"What's the matter?" he asked. "A minute ago you were lordly as a hog on ice, and now you don't look so good. Has your memory gone back on you?"

Simon came back with pencil and paper and shoved them impatiently at Stanley. "Here. Get busy. We haven't all the time in creation."

"Time," said Stanley. "If Comyn hadn't interfered—"

"A very odd thing has happened," said Peter slowly. "I'm beginning to like Comyn. We have much in common."

Stanley threw the pencil on the floor. "I can't do it here," he said. "Nobody could. I'm going to my cabin and it may take me a little while. Don't disturb me. If there's any more trouble made for me, you'll all pay for it."

He stamped out. Nobody spoke until he was gone, and then Comyn said:

"Don't blow a fuse. If anything goes wrong, this paper can be pieced together again. I was careful how I tore it."

Simon said, "He couldn't have got the log books aboard. I examined every piece of baggage myself."

"Not the books themselves," said Comyn. "But a couple of micro-photostats could slide by in a pack of cigarettes or a roll of socks."

"Well," said Simon, "let's go."

"Give him a while," said Peter. "Let him get set. I'll need the master key. Those metal doors don't break open very easy."

They waited a little, and then the three of them went very quietly through the main cabin, where there were still clusters of men by the ports, and down the passageway to Stanley's cabin. Peter nodded and put the key into the lock.

The door swung in. It had taken only a few seconds to open it, but Stanley must have been sitting inside with his reflexes on hair-triggers, listening, fearing, hoping, not knowing whether to delay or to hurry, and not daring to do either. There was a large ash tray on his table with a tiny fire burning in it, and Comyn saw the finish of an action that must have started with the first touch of the key to the lock. A roll of microfilm dropped into the fire, flared, and was gone, and Stanley was already scrabbling for the other one, the one he had been copying from. But he couldn't pick it up so easily because it was pinned under a small but very powerful lens.

Comyn sprang forward. Peter and Simon were right with him. They hit Stanley almost together, bore him over and fell in a sprawling undignified tangle, six hands clawing for the tiny thing that Stanley had tight in his clenched fist. Comyn got his hands around Stanley's wrist and squeezed. Peter was saying. "Look out, don't tear it!" and Stanley was trying to fend them all off with one hand and his feet. He was sobbing like a woman and cursing them. Finally Simon hit him in the face. He went limp for a moment and his fingers relaxed and Peter got the film.

They rolled off each other and got up, leaving Stanley sitting on the floor with one hand to the side of his face where Simon had struck him. There was a smear of blood at the corner of his mouth. Peter looked down at him. He was breathing hard and his eyes were ugly. He said to Simon:

"Get that paper off him."

Simon began to search him, roughly. Stanley said, "No!" on a high rising note, and floundered up. He swung at Simon's head and missed, and Simon hit him again, openhanded this time, contemptuously, but hard. "Stop it," he said, "or I'll break your jaw." Peter stepped up and held Stanley's arms from behind. Simon found the paper.

"Give it here," said Peter. He let go of Stanley and took the paper. The fire was still smoldering in the big ash tray. He put Stanley's guarantee of empire into it and watched it burn.

Stanley said, "You can't do that. It isn't that easy." His voice was high. He wiped with the back of his hand at the blood on his mouth. "The other roll is gone—the last book, the one about the Transuranae. I still know what's in it. You can't get along without me."

The ashes crumbled and turned gray. Peter Cochrane said slowly, "We'll get along, Bill. You're not a big enough man to bull us out, and you know it. It's time you stopped being a fool."

"What do you expect me to do?" asked Stanley savagely. "Agree with you?"

"I'm going to make you a proposition," Peter said. "I will give you, in your own name, a fair share of Cochrane Transuranic—and no more than a fair share, no more than any of the others who volunteered for this trip will get. Furthermore, Simon and I will agree to forget your recent behavior."

Stanley laughed. "That's big of you. Listen, in a little while you'll be landing on Barnard II. Unless I tell you what was in that book, the same thing will happen to you that happened to Rogers and Vickrey and Strang and Kessel—and Ballantyne. You don't dare take that chance."

Comyn had started forward at the mention of Rogers' name, but Peter stopped him.

"Let me do this . . . All right, Bill, so it happens to us, and it doesn't happen to you. Where will you be? Can you pick up the pieces of the expedition and take the survivors home—or if there aren't any, go back by yourself? There's more to a bluff than words. There's got to be a man to back it up."

Stanley said between his teeth, "You're not doing so well with *your* bluff. The fact you're willing to make concessions at all shows that—"

Peter's hand shot out and gripped the front of Stanley's shirt.

"Get one thing through your head," said Peter in a very soft voice. "I'm making no concessions to you. I'm thinking of Claudia. Be thankful you're married to a Cochrane, for if you weren't I'd throw you to the hogs."

He flung him off with such fierce contempt that Stanley stumbled and half fell onto the edge of his bunk.

"Now, you cheap little chiseler," said Peter, "do you want your job back or don't you?"

Stanley was still sitting on the edge of his bunk. He looked at Peter fixedly, and then answered him in four vicious words.

He added, "I've still got you in a cleft stick. You've got to know about the Transuranae and what else is on that world. You'll pay for that knowledge, or you'll get what Ballantyne got."

Peter said harshly, "I've known you a long time, Bill. You're a tough man behind a desk, but not anywhere else. You'll take the share I offered you and be glad of it."

He turned away. Comyn's fists itched, but he followed. Stanley shouted furiously after them:

"A share in Cochrane Transuranic you'll give me! That's funny, that's very funny. You don't know what the hell you're giving out shares in but you will, you will—"

Comyn slammed the door. Peter scowled down at the roll of microfilm in his hand. "That's what old Jonas meant by amateurs who bungle unpredictably. But one thing sure, he's scared. He's plenty scared, and not of us."

Three days later they were in an orbit around Barnard II, and going down.

XI

COMYN SLEPT, a light, uneasy, restless sleep. His dreams were full of voices, full of words and pictures: the landing; the grassy plain, with the strange slim golden trees; the mountains to the south, the tall cliffs and rocky spires, tortured by wind and water into shapes that leaned and crouched and made to spring; the gorge that cleft them.

There had been the land and the day of waiting, penned inside the ship, while the endless tests were made. Finally it was determined: "No contamination of the air." Stanley's face set like marble, Stanley's mouth unspeaking. "You'll have to pay me, Peter. You'll have to pay."

Men going out, wearing armor, carrying Geigers. No radiation, no contamination, not here on the plain. Men could come out and breathe again. It was safe.

Peter staring off toward the mountains. "Is it there?"

Stanley saying, "I'll tell you, but you'll have to pay."

"Tomorrow . . ."

"If you pay."

Dreams, oppressive, somber, filled with beauty, tinged with fear. Beauty of wild tree and sweeping plain, beauty of sound and color—all alien, new and strange. Comyn tossed in the narrow bunk and saw again the mountains and the gorge as he had seen them at the going-down of Barnard's Star, a rust-red giant heavy in the west. Red light poured down on the world, the screaming spires dripping blood from off their flanks. They were beautiful even then, beautiful as battle, as armed knights clashing above the shadowed gorge.

And then in the dream was sunset, and the coming on of night. Dusk and darkness, and underneath them horror. Horror that sped through the golden trees, faster and faster on noiseless feet, calling, crying, toward the ship, "*I am Paul. I am dead, but I cannot die!*"

Comyn woke with a leap and a yell. He was shaking,

drenched with sweat. The cabin was filled with moonlight that came in through the port, but the room was small and close and he had seen too much of its walls. It felt like a coffin, and nightmares clung in its corners. He went out of it and down the passage.

The lock was open. A man sat inside of it, with a high-powered shock-rifle on his lap.

"I'm going out," said Comyn.

The man looked at him doubtfully. "I have my orders," he said. "But the old man's out there. You ask him."

Comyn stepped through the round thick walled opening and climbed down the ladder. Two copper moons burned in the sky, and a third was rising huge and tawny from the horizon. There was no darkness except where the groves of slender trees trailed it from their boughs. A little to the left, still plain under the returning grass, were the scar and the hollow where Ballantyne's ship had lain.

Peter Cochrane was walking back and forth by the foot of the ladder. He stopped and spoke:

"I'm glad you came. It isn't good to be alone on a strange world." He took Comyn's arm and pulled him away a little, out of the glow from the ship's ports. "Look off there, straight down the gorge. Is that just moonlight?"

"Hard to say. . . ." The three moons wove a tapestry of light that glanced and gleamed in a bewildering way, shifting constantly and very bright. But Comyn thought he saw, down among the cliffs where Peter was pointing, a pale white fire not made by any moon. It was a fragile, glittering aurora that set his nerves to leaping with an awareness of the unknown . . . and then vanished from his dazzled eyes, lost in the overwhelming moonlight.

"I don't know," said Comyn. "I can't be sure."

"That's the devil of it," Peter said. "We're not sure of anything."

He started to walk back toward the ship. Comyn followed him. From somewhere in the night behind them came a soft fluting call, very clear and sweet, with a sound in it like laughter. Peter jerked his head toward it.

"Take that, for instance. What is it—bird, beast, something with no name at all? Who knows?"

"Stanley might. What are you going to do about Stanley?"

"Comyn, there are times when only a damn fool won't give in. This may be one of them. I don't know." He shook his head somberly. "If it were just myself and Simon, I'd see him in blazes first. But I can't take that chance with the others."

He glanced around the moon-washed plain. "I look at this place, and I think there can't be any danger here. Regular Garden of Eden, isn't it? And then I remember Ballantyne, and I'm willing to give Stanley the whole Cochrane Corporation if he can give us only a hint of how to save ourselves from what happened to him."

"But you don't really think he can."

"I don't know, Comyn. But I do know nobody else can."

"So you'll come to terms with him."

"Probably," said Peter, as though the word tasted bitter in his mouth.

Again the bird-like call came, very soft this time, but sounding much closer. There was a grove of trees perhaps sixty yards away. The two men turned toward it, curious to see if possible what sort of creature was there, singing in the night. The shadows underneath the boughs were dark, but the coppery moonlight shafted down in the open spaces. Comyn saw a flicker of movement.

Peter's hand closed hard upon his arm. "Men! Do you see them, Comyn? Human—"

The words choked in his throat. Suddenly night and distance were not, and Comyn saw clearly the ivory bodies stealing between the trees. His dream was still strong in him. He tore away from Peter's grasp and began to run out across the plain, shouting, "Paul! Paul Rogers!" And it was like the nightmare in reverse. The long grass plucked at his feet and the trees seemed far away, and the faces of the men beneath them were obscured. Men, four men, Ballantyne's crew— No, there were more than four. The grove was full of slim pale bodies, naked, light of foot, and some of them were not men at all. He could see even at that distance that they were women, with long hair blowing as they ran. And they were running now. They were frightened by his shouting, and the grove rang with fluting calls, a kind of speech, but very simple, like the speech of birds.

He cried, "Paul, don't run away. It's me, Arch Comyn!"

But the white bodies vanished between the shadows and the trees, back into the deeper woods beyond, and Paul was not there. And the clear full-throated calling died away and was gone.

Peter caught him just on the edge of the grove. "Don't go in there, Comyn!"

Comyn shook his head. "Gone now. I scared them off. It wasn't Paul. It wasn't any of them." A long sliding shiver racked him, and his breath came hard. "Peter, do you think those people are the . . . Transuranae?"

Men were coming out from the ship now, roused by the shouting and the calls. Peter turned abruptly. "Stanley," he said. "Now is the time to talk to Stanley."

Comyn followed him, still half dazed, oppressed with a sense of loss and a desire not to be near that grove of slender trees. The wind blew warm, laden with nameless scents, and in the sky were foreign constellations made pallid by the moons. The voices of the men rose loud and harsh, spreading outward from the ship.

He saw Peter call four men and give them rapid orders, pointing to the grove. The men had rifles. They moved past Comyn, and one of them, a big fellow named Fisher, said:

"Are they armed? Are they going to attack?"

"I don't think so. They seemed to be . . . just looking."

Fisher's face had sweat on it, and his shirt was dark under the arms. He wiped his sleeve across his mouth and glanced without love at the shadows under the boughs.

"This trip had better pay off," he said. "I haven't liked it so far."

He started on, and Comyn said, "Don't take any chances."

Fisher said profanely that he would not.

By the time Comyn reached the ship the four had vanished into the edge of the grove. He did not envy the men their posts as sentinels.

There was a small group around the foot of the ladder. Peter and Stanley were the core of it. The others watched and listened, nervous men, unhappy men, not liking the night.

Peter was saying, "Let's get this straight now. I want everybody to understand. You refuse to tell us what you know about these . . . people, whether they're dangerous or not?"

Stanley slid the end of his tongue across his lips, which were pale and dry. "Not for nothing, Peter. If anything happens it'll be your fault, not mine, because you wouldn't make a fair deal."

"He refuses," Peter said to the men who were listening. "You all heard that."

There was a mutter of assent. It had an ugly tone beneath it, and Stanley turned, as though he would go back inside the ship.

The men closed in, barring his way. Peter said, "All right, let's take him out there."

Several of them took hold of Stanley. Simon Cochrane, one of the pilots, an astrophysicist, French the doctor, others. They had stopped being scientists or experts, men with important jobs. They were just men now, afraid and angry. Stanley cried out.

Peter slapped him across the mouth, not hard. "You wouldn't believe this, Bill, but it's the principle of the thing. The stuff about the landing was for money. This is for lives. There's a difference. I don't like being blackmailed for peoples' lives." He started out across the plain. "Bring him along."

They brought him. Comyn went with them. He knew what Peter was going to do, and so did Stanley, but Stanley asked.

"Nothing," said Peter. "Just tie you to a tree in the grove and then drop back a way and see what happens. If you have all this knowledge you claim to have you know whether there's any danger or not. If there isn't you won't be afraid, and nothing will happen to you. If there is—well, we'll find that out too."

Stanley's feet dragged in the long grass. But they took him into the edge of the grove, under the first fringe of golden boughs that were tarnished copper now in the moonlight. There was silence between the trees and patches of gliding light and a little wind that whispered.

"Not here," said Peter. "Further in."

Deeper in were more of the slender trunks and beyond them was the forest, the dark forest that lay between them and the mountains. The forest where the unknown ones had gone.

They treaded softly, shock-guns ready, their eyes searching every shadow with caution and alarm. Five steps, ten, twenty—and Stanley broke.

"Don't do it, Peter! Don't leave me here! I don't know . . . *I don't know!*"

Peter stopped. He pulled Stanley into a drift of moonlight and studied his face.

"I don't know," Stanley said miserably. "Ballantyne described these—these people. He met them, all right. But that's all he said about them in the log."

Comyn asked, "Are they the Transuranae?"

"I suppose so. He didn't name them. He just said they were here."

"Was he afraid of them?"

"He didn't say so."

"What did he say?"

"That was all. He told what the place was like, all the tests they ran, then about the people and then the log ended. He never made any more entries. Except one."

"Go on."

"It was only one word and it wasn't finished. It was in ink, all over the page: TRANSURAN—" Stanley shut his teeth tight on the beginning of unhealthy laughter. "It was that one unfinished word that made me take the logbooks. I thought I had the Cochrane fortune right there. And then Ballantyne himself gave that part of it away. Let's get out of here, Peter. Let's get back to the ship."

"Then you were lying," said Peter mercilessly. "when you said you knew the location of the ores."

Stanley nodded.

Peter studied him a moment longer. Then he turned and walked back through the grove. The others followed. Peter spoke briefly to the sentinels. They passed out onto the plain again, onto the path of trampled grass. Stanley walked a little apart. They were not holding him now.

Some of the men were already back inside the ship when lightning began to flash and crack among the trees. A man yelled, high and shrill with fright, and there was a sudden bursting-forth of the bird-like calls. This time a single note repeated, receding away into the forest. It was a note of lamentation. The bolts of lightning flared and flared, the wild discharge of panic.

Presently all quieted. The single mourning note had faded to a distant wail that lost itself against the mountains. Fisher and another man came out of the grove, dragging a limp white form between them.

"They tried to rush us," Fisher yelled. "They were coming, but we drove 'em off." His face shone with clammy moisture and his voice was ragged. "We got one still alive."

Once more Comyn crossed the stretch of plain toward the woods. He walked beside Peter, his eyes fixed on the naked body that dragged from the sweaty hands of Fisher and his mate. The head hung forward, hidden by a fall of dark hair. He could not see the face.

They met in the center of the open space. Fisher grunted and the body rolled onto the grass. Comyn drew his hand across his face and looked down.

Peter drew a long, unsteady breath. "I know that man," he said in an oddly stilted way. "It's Vickrey."

XII

THE SHIP's small hospital was a cubicle of brilliant light, sterile, white, barbed with glints of chromium and surgical steel. Vickrey lay on the table. He had caught the edge of a shock-beam, and he had not yet returned to consciousness. French was working over him, his rubber-gloved hands touching Vickrey with a curious reluctance, his mouth drawn down to a narrow line. On Vickrey's arm was a patch of tape, covering the place whence a tissue sample had been taken.

Comyn stood out of the way, with his back against the wall, and watched. Time and countless millions of miles and many events rolled back, and he was in another hospital room on another world, and another man lay before him unconscious. Again he saw the subtle rippling and motion of the flesh, as though the body cells had an unnatural life of their own. And he was sick.

Peter Cochrane whispered, "Ballantyne was like that."

Comyn answered, "When I first saw him. Before he was . . . dead."

Peter stood beside Comyn. Their shoulders touched in the cramped space. It seemed very hot and close under the glaring lights, and yet they felt cold. Vickrey breathed. His face was closed and secret, and his body stirred: the muscles, the tendons, the thin covering flesh. He was not wasted and worn as Ballantyne had been; there was a health to his leanness.

Peter whispered, "He's changed. He looks younger. I don't understand that."

Roth came back into the hospital from his laboratory and laid a written report on French's desk. "I tested the tissue sample," he said. "It's the same as Ballantyne's, except that the concentration of transuranic elements is greater. Much greater."

"Quiet," French said. "He's coming round."

96

Silence. The man on the table turned his head and sighed. After a minute he opened his eyes. They looked first, with a vague curiosity, at the low white ceiling, and then at the white walls and the cases of bright instruments, and then at the men who stood near. The vague curiosity sharpened into alarm, into terror, into the look of a stunned wild thing that wakes to find a cage around it. Vickrey sat up on the table and cried out—a shrill-edged fluting call, infinitely strange to come from the throat of an Earthman.

Peter said, "Vickrey. Vickrey, it's all right, we're friends."

Again the desperate call, the unhuman cry for help. It set Comyn's nerves on edge, but it was not as bad as Vickrey's face—an ordinary face, an Earthman's face, but altered and made alien, the mouth distorted in the forming of that wild cry, the eyes . . .

The eyes. Comyn was not an especially imaginative man, and he could not have said what it was about Vickrey's eyes that made them abnormal and frightening in a man's face. There was no menace in them and no madness; it was not any overt quality. It was something else, something lacking. He caught their direct stare and it jarred him in a queer way that set the hairs to prickling on the back of his neck.

Peter said again, "Vickrey! You remember me, Peter Cochrane. You're safe now, Vickrey. You're all right. Don't be afraid."

For a third time the bird-like calling came incongruously from the lips of a mathematician who had once had a wife and children and a position in the world of science.

Abruptly, Peter swore. "Come off it, Vickrey. You're not one of those creatures. You're an Earthman, and you know who I am. Stop pretending."

Vickrey moaned.

Comyn asked the question he had asked before, of another man, in another room. "Where is Paul Rogers?"

Vickrey turned his head and looked at Comyn with those fey eyes, and after a long time he spoke, in words so difficult and slurred that they were hardly English.

He said, "It was Strang you killed."

Peter Cochrane started. "Strang! Was he—"

"In the grove. Men with guns. Strang fell. We picked him up and started away. Then I—" He shook his head. His hair had grown long and there were bits of leaf and grass in it from where he had been rolled on the ground.

Peter said slowly, "The men said you attacked them."

Vickrey made a sound that might have been a laugh or a sob. "No," he said. "No. We didn't even see them."

There was a hot and sudden light in Peter's eyes. "Those bloody fools," he said. "Panic. Sheer panic. I shouldn't have sent them out there."

Comyn said to Vickrey, "We came here partly to find you. Were you trying to come back?"

"No!" Vickrey put his elbows on his knees, raised his hands and laid his head between them. "We stayed behind. We thought that men might try to take us back. But the People wanted to see the ship. We waited, and then someone shouted, shouted Rogers' name and another, and Rogers heard. And he wanted to look at the man who shouted. So after a while we four crept back into the grove. I didn't have to. I guess I was—" Once more he stopped in mid-sentence. Presently he said, with infinite sadness, "Strang is dead."

"I'm sorry," Peter said. "The men didn't mean to. They were scared by all the talk about the Transuranae."

Vickrey straightened up, as sharply as though someone had touched him with a knife. "What do you know about the Transuranae?"

"Nothing, except what Ballantyne wrote in his log."

"But he didn't keep the log after—" Vickrey stood up. His strength seemed to have come back to him with amazing swiftness. "Ballantyne! He got back to Earth, then."

Peter nodded.

"And," said Vickrey, "he died."

"Yes. Did you know he would?"

"Of course. We all knew. But he was too crazy, too inhibited, too afraid to take what the Transuranae had given him. He would not stay."

"What had they given him, Vickrey?"

"Life," said Vickrey. "Life or death, and he made up his own mind. He didn't think it was decent to live."

"I don't understand you."

"If you did, you'd be like me, like Ballantyne. You'd have the choice to make, too. Listen, take your ship and your men and go very fast. Forget that Rogers and Kessel and I ever existed on Earth. Find another star, space is full of them. Otherwise, it'll be as it was with us. Most of you will stay, but some will go back and—yes, I can see in your faces. It was a very ugly death."

For the first time French spoke. He had been reading Roth's report, looking from it to Vickrey, and thinking hard.

"It's a change, isn't it?" he said. "It wasn't complete in Ballantyne."

"A change," said Vickrey. "Yes. Ballantyne left too soon. He—it horrified him, somehow. Too much the puritan, I guess, at heart. And yet if he had waited . . ."

French said, "It's complete in you."

Vickrey didn't answer that. Instead he looked at Peter Cochrane and said, "You'll let me go? You're not going to take me back to Earth?"

Peter put out his hand in what was almost a gesture of pleading. "You can't stay here forever with these primitives. You're an Earthman, Vickrey. You have a career, a wife and children. I know you've been under some strange influence here, but you'll come out of it. And whatever your, well, your illness may be, medical attention—"

Vickrey cut him short with a cry. "Illness! No, you don't understand! I'm not ill, I can never be ill. I can be injured, I can be killed. But those are accidents, and barring them I can live—not forever, but close enough to it that the human mind is not conscious of the difference."

He came up to Peter Cochrane, and there was fear in him, a desperate fear. "I belong here now. You can't force me to go back."

"Listen," said Peter, trying hard to be gentle. "When you first came to, you couldn't remember how to talk. Now your speech is as clear as mine. It'll all come back to you just as easily, the old ways, your own ways. And your wife . . ."

Vickrey smiled. "She was good to me. I'm not sure I ever loved her. But we'd have no use for each other now." Then the fear came back and he cried out, "Let me go!"

Peter sighed. "I think you'd better stay here and rest a while. You'll feel differently in a day or two. Besides, we need your help."

"I'll help you," Vickrey said. "I'll tell you anything you want—but you must let me go!"

Peter shook his head. "You'd bolt off into the forest and be gone with the Transuranae again, and we'd never find you."

Vickrey was still for a long minute and then he began to laugh. And the laughter slipped off shockingly into one of those eerie calls, a double note that trailed away in a throbbing minor wail. Peter reached out and shook him.

"Stop it," he said. "Stop acting like a fool."

Vickrey caught his breath. "You think my people—you think *they* are the Transuranae?"

"Aren't they?"

"No." Vickrey shook off Peter's grasp and turned away, his hands clenched now into fists, his naked body quivering with tension. "I know what you want. We wanted them too. The transuranic ores. But you can't get them. It isn't possible! They already belong."

"To what?"

"To the Transuranae. And I tell you to leave them alone. But you won't."

"No. We're better equipped than you were. We can handle anything, if we just know what to expect. What are the Transuranae like? Are they people, beasts, what?"

Vickrey looked at him, almost in pity. "They are nothing you ever dreamed of," he said softly. "And they're nothing I can describe or explain. Let me go now. I can't stand being shut up like this. I'll point out the way for you to their place, where the ores are. Let me go."

"You know I can't do that," Peter said. "For your own sake, and for the others too, Rogers and Kessel."

"You can't understand," whispered Vickrey. "You *won't* understand that we can't go back among men. We don't want to go back!"

His voice, on those last words, had risen to a kind of scream, and French said worriedly, "Be careful, Peter."

Comyn said, "I think Vickrey's telling the truth." He

stepped forward casually, so that he stood between Peter Cochrane and the door. "And I think you're handing him a lot of crumbs for the birds. I don't think you care about his sake or Rogers' or Kessel's, one way or the other. All you want is the ores, and you're afraid to turn him loose to lead you there—he might just disappear. So you're going to—"

Behind him, so suddenly that the edge of it hit him before he could get out of the way, the door opened. Simon Cochrane had been outside the ship in command of the guard detail, and now he stood in the opening, his rifle still in his hand, his face intent and nervous.

"Peter," he said, "you'd better come—and bring *him* along too." He nodded to Vickrey and then pointed off in the direction of the mountains. "There's something going on out there."

XIII

ONE OF the moons had set, and the shadows were deeper in the distant gorge. The breeze had quieted, and the night was warm and very still. Simon held up his hand.

"Listen," he said.

They listened, and in the stillness Comyn heard the sound of many voices, sweet and far off among the dark feet of the mountains, calling, answering, drawing together from the groves and the forests and the moon-washed plains.

"They're gathering," Simon said. "Ask him what it means."

The sweet unhuman voices called. And now from a point about the mouth of the gorge, more and more of them began to join together, and a cold quiver shot down Comyn's spine. He had heard that before, that double note that died away in a minor wailing.

Vickrey's face was a mask of anguished longing, lifting up in the moonlight. He said, "They are taking Strang to his burial." He tried desperately to break away, but he was between Peter and Simon, and they held him.

"Where?" said Peter. "To the place of the Transuranae?" Deep in the shadowed throat of the gorge the pale white fire showed brighter now, bright enough to be seen and recognized as something separate from the moonlight. The voices were moving slowly toward it.

Vickrey said, "You've killed once, you'll kill again. You'll take the others prisoner as you took me. Let me go!"

He fought and strained like a mad thing, but they held him and others came to help. And Vickrey's voice rose in a shrill wild cry. Comyn moved away to one side.

Simon said disgustedly, "He's no good to us. Lock him up until he comes to his senses. Anyway, we don't dare go now while the whole lot of them are there. They'll want to make us pay for Strang, and there's too many of them."

The sentinels had been called in from the grove. Fisher stood looking uneasily from the mountains to the turmoil around Vickrey. Comyn walked up behind him, making no sound on the grass. He hit Fisher on the side of the jaw and took the rifle out of his hand as he went down. The stud was pushed up to full power. Comyn eased it back and then he turned to the group of men who were struggling with Vickrey.

"All right," he said. "Let him go."

They didn't let him go, not at once. It was a minute before they understood why they had to. Vickrey was on his knees, and Simon had hold of him. Peter Cochrane straightened up.

"Are you crazy, Comyn?"

"Maybe." Someone went for the rifle he had dropped in the scuffle, and Comyn pressed the firing stud. There was a sharp flash and the man went down. After that nobody made trouble. Getting knocked cold might not be fatal, but it was no fun. Simon still held onto Vickrey. He was so close to him that Comyn couldn't knock him out without hitting Vickrey too. Simon Cochrane's jaw was stubborn and his eyes were mean.

Comyn said, "Let him go."

Peter came forward a step or two. He started to speak, and Comyn cut him short. "Listen," he said, "I don't give a curse about the ores or whether you get them or not. I came out here to find Paul Rogers, and that's all I care about. Do you understand that, Vickrey? I'm Paul's friend. I want to talk to him, and that's all. If he doesn't want to go back, I won't try to make him. Will you take me to him?"

Vickrey nodded. He tried to pull away from Simon, and Simon struck him. "Stay put," Simon said, and then he shouted to the men who were standing around, "What's the matter with you? Somebody take care of that—"

Peter's hand caught his collar, choked off his words and his wind with them. "Get up," Peter snarled. He dragged Simon away from Vickrey and thrust him aside, viciously. "You never know when to quit, do you? You're the kind of Cochrane that's given the whole family a bad name. This is no place for rough stuff, not with him."

Simon swore. "You told me not to let him get away."

"I didn't tell you to beat him up." He swung around.

"You can put the gun down, Comyn. Vickrey's free to do what he wants. I guess he was telling the truth, and it is too late to help him. There's no use killing a man trying to save his life."

Comyn smiled and shook his head. He did not put the gun down. "I can't make you out," he said to Peter. "Sometimes I think you're a decent guy, and sometimes I think you're a heel with a genius for covering up." He moved the barrel of the rifle up and down gently, just to remind Peter that it was still there. "I need armor."

"You must be crazy! Comyn, you can't—"

"You know me well enough to know I'm going, whether I have the armor or not. And I know you well enough to know you'll get it for me. So let's not waste any more time."

Peter shrugged and turned away to the ship. Simon started to follow him, and Comyn said, "No. You stay here, where I can watch you."

He waited. Vickrey had risen to his feet. There was a new look about him now. He was free and he wasn't afraid any longer. His body quivered, but it was with eagerness, and his gaze was on the mountains, on the shadowed gorge where the voices called. His eyes shone, and again Comyn wondered when he saw them why they were so unhuman, so changed from the eyes of man.

Peter came back, carrying a suit of the flexible radiation armor done up in a bulky pack, with the helmet on top. There was a hard set to his mouth, and his glance probed angrily around at the men's faces.

"One of these is missing," he said. "Somebody's beat you to it, Comyn."

"Put it down," said Comyn. "Right there." Peter laid the pack on the ground and stepped back, and Comyn picked it up. Simon was still sulking. He did not speak, but Peter asked:

"Has anybody seen Bill Stanley?"

No one had.

Peter said some hot and angry words. "Amateurs! That goes for you too, Comyn. Things aren't hard enough, you all have to foul things up for everybody grinding your own little axes. All right, get the hell on with it, and I hope you both fall into a chasm and break your necks!"

"Then don't follow too close behind me," Comyn said. "Come on, Vickrey."

Vickrey spoke, suddenly, clearly. He was speaking to Peter Cochrane, and there was in him all the dignity of a free man, a man of science. There was something else, too, that made them feel small and a little unclean before him, an inexplicable and irritating sensation to come from a naked creature who had gone native in some weird way.

"I know that you will follow," he said. "The light is there in the gorge, and there will be many on the trails. What will happen to you afterward is partly in your hands. I only warn you not to make the mistake that Ballantyne did —and not to use your rifles on my people. Strang is dead, and they will mourn him for a short while. But there is no vengeance in them. They have forgotten vengeance, along with many other things that they once knew. Do not harm them. They are harmless."

Without looking at any of them again, Vickrey set off across the plain. Comyn went after him, and presently the shadows of the grove wrapped around them. Vickrey sped on, and the voices called in the distance, and Comyn threw the gun away. Vickrey smiled.

"You're wiser than the Cochranes."

Comyn grunted. "There are times when a gun doesn't help. I just got a feeling this was one of them."

"Are you afraid?"

"Yes," said Comyn. "There used to be a dirty saying for just how scared I am." They were through the grove now and in among the forest trees, great trees with blackness around their feet. The tangled boughs above Comyn's head were not like any he had seen before except in dreams, and the leaves on them hung in strange curling shapes, copper and gold and pallid silver under the moons. The moist sod gave off strange scents where he crushed it under his boots, and there were vines with huge dark flowers. Vickrey moved swiftly and without sound, a slim white blur in the gloom, and it was like running with a ghost.

As they went, Comyn asked, "What about your people? You said they used to be men, like—"

He caught himself, but Vickrey smiled and finished it for him. "Like me. Yes. Barnard's Star has eight worlds. They came from the fifth one, originally, moving closer in toward their sun as it waned. In the course of ages they reached this planet and found the Transuranae. They will not travel any more."

Thinking of the shapes that had run faun-like through the grove, naked and lacking even speech except for those simple calls, Comyn asked incredulously, "You mean those— you mean *they had spaceships?*"

"Oh, yes. Spaceships and great cities and war and medicine and politics—civilization. There are ruins beyond the mountains of the cities they built when they first came to Barnard II. Fine ones too. I've seen them. Their culture was on approximately the same level as our own." He shook his head. "It's becoming difficult for me to think of such things. The mind adjusts so easily to altered ideas of importance."

After a moment he added, "I wish your ship hadn't come. It's unhappy to try being Vickrey again."

Comyn noted the odd choice of words, but he didn't mention it. Instead he said, breathing hard, "Don't you ever get tired?"

Vickrey made a gesture of impatience, but he slowed down to a walk. Comyn plodded gratefully for a while until his heart quit hammering and the sweat rolled less violently down his back, where the armor-pack weighed heavily. They were closer to the gorge now, and the voices sounded clearer, like the voices of great birds. They seemed to hold no menace, and yet the very feyness of them was terrifying—perhaps because it should have been insane and wasn't.

"How did they lose it all?" he asked. "The spaceships and the cities. Civilization."

"I told you. They found the Transuranae."

"War?" said Comyn.

Vickrey looked at him as though he had said a childish thing. "Not war. No. It was only a question of need."

"Of need?"

"Yes. Everything man has ever done has been done out of need—for food, for shelter, for mutual protection. Civilization developed to supply those necessities easily. But if they're no longer necessary to you, you have developed beyond civilization and can slough it off."

"You mean that those things are no longer necessary to you, Vickrey? Because of their weird transuranic poisoning?"

"It's not poisoning, it's transmutation. A complete physiological *change*, where ordinary metabolism ceases to be and is replaced by energy, a constant flow of it through the living cells from the transuranic elements those cells have ingested. The body has a new self-sufficient life. It has no hunger and no fear. So the brain that is in it has no longer any use for cities, for finance and intricate social structures, for work and gain, for war and greed—not even for complicated speech. They sound ridiculous here, don't they, all those pompous words?"

There was a curious sickness in Comyn, a shivering recoil from an unimaginable kind of living thus unfolded.

"But radioactive matter kills," he said.

"The elements we knew on Earth, yes. But they're the end-products, the embers, still burning and with a long way yet to the ultimate lead, but with their vital energy gone. Neptunium and plutonium are hybrids, man-made and unnatural. The true transuranics, far and far beyond our periodic table, are the forces that were in the beginning, the life seeds, the fountainhead. Perhaps we're all children of the Transuranae in a way, many times removed and with all our vital powers gone too."

"I don't understand."

"You will," said Vickrey. "Can you run now? There is still a way to go."

Even while he spoke he was forgetting Comyn and the things that he had talked about, straining toward the gorge. Comyn ran.

And as he ran, the fear in him deepened—the fear of a tough-minded man who felt all his hard, matter-of-fact certitudes suddenly threatened, his familiar world quaking around him.

"But if the Transuranae worked that change in you, who are they?" he cried.

Vickrey did not answer. The ground was sloping upward and they had come into a broad path between the trees, trodden by many feet over countless years, so that it was worn deep below the level of the sod and packed as hard as iron. Vickrey was speeding faster along it, and Comyn labored after him. He could see the gorge now through the thinning forest, dark, dark under the slanting moons. The voices rang.

There were others on the path.

Vickrey called, a gentle, joyous note, and they answered him—the slender people, the child-eyed people who looked at Comyn and were puzzled, but only a little afraid. He went up with them toward the mouth of the gorge. He kept close to Vickrey because he knew if he lost him he would bolt and run. He could not have stood to be alone among these creatures who looked like men and women and were not.

The last trees dropped behind them. They streamed up between the stony pinnacles that were the pillars of the gate, and the gorge lay open before them. It was full of voices and dim moving shapes, and forward in its deep cleft the white fire burned, as snow burns under a brilliant sun. Vickrey paused and said one dreaming word. Human speech was slipping from him now.

Comyn put on the clumsy armor and set the helmet over his head. And he was afraid.

It was worse now, with the ray-proof metal fabric hampering his limbs and the face-plate of leaded glass cutting down his field of vision. Sweat soaked his clothing, and the canned, flat air from the shielded tank between his shoulders was difficult to breathe.

He stumbled after Vickrey along a path worn smooth and broad across the rock. There were bodies all around him now, naked bodies. Many of them were women with white thighs and pointed breasts, but they roused in him no lust, and the men gave him no sense of shame. It seemed as natural that they should go unclothed as it was for the winds to blow.

They were hurrying and their faces were bright. The sound of voices was dying away as fewer and fewer were left on the open path. The wild tortured shapes of rock sprang up on either side, with heads and shoulders bathed in ruddy moonlight. But that was high above. Where Comyn was the darkness clustered thick, and there was no light except that strange white fire that drew and beckoned. Some infection began to enter into him from Vickrey and the others, so that he too was eager to reach it. But with every step he took toward the fire, the fear in him grew greater.

The floor of the gorge dipped downward steeply and the path went with it, and a great ragged grotto opened in the rock. The white fire came out of it, but Comyn saw now that the radiance he had been watching was only a fragment of what lay inside. The path split and curved away to left and right, in along the sides of the grotto, and the last of the people streamed along the two paths. Comyn stopped.

"Vickrey!" he cried out. "Vickrey!"

But Vickrey was gone. Comyn took hold of the rock wall beside him with his two hands and clung to it for a while. He stood just at the edge of the grotto, neither in nor out, until he decided whether he was going to run away or not. And he saw the reason why the path split.

The floor of the grotto was cracked wide open in a rough-edged chasm. Through this crack the white light poured upward: an aurora of blinding purity, with a rippling in it. The lips of the chasm and the grotto roof above, where the light struck most strongly, burned with their own dimmer fires. And Comyn thought that ages of intense bombardment by transuranic radiation had transmuted the common rock into something else, so that the whole grotto was filled with radiance.

He could not see in the chasm; he was too far from it and the angle was wrong. But he could see the ledges on either side, the lower ones wide, the upper ones climbing the grotto walls in rough steps. They were crowded now with the people whose eyes were so disturbing, and they had the happy faces of children at a festival. At one place a part of the lower ledge thrust out a little over the crack, and here there was a long litter made of rude poles and heaped high with flowers. The flowers moved and stirred with the motion of the thing they covered, and beside the litter stood two men. Between the distance and the dazzle, Comyn could not make out their faces. But he knew one of them.

He took his hands away from the rock, set his teeth hard and went into the grotto.

XIV

THE PEOPLE were still in motion, and he moved with them, an incongruous lumbering shape among the lithe bare bodies. The wide lower ledges were filled. But on the others that rose like rough steps above them, winding and tilting along the sides of the grotto, the people were streaming up, a shifting fresco of white forms, silent-footed, eager. There was a stillness in the place and a sense of some unknown power crouched and waiting to leap forth. They were waiting for it; they had known it before, and Comyn ran heavily along the crowded ledge toward Paul Rogers. He did not wish to see the leaping forth, and time was pressing on him like a spur. The white fires rushed upward from the chasm, a glory and a fear.

He shouted Paul's name, but his voice was muffled by the helmet. And the men on the jutting lip of rock were lost in some far distance of their own. They stooped and lifted up the bier that held Strang's body, and a cascade of brilliant flowers fell from it to the ground.

The streaming of the people onto the upper ledges quickened. Comyn's armored boots struck heavy on the rock.

Slowly, very solemnly, the men lowered the foot of Strang's rude bier and let the body slip, still stirring, into the abyss.

The motion of the people ceased. There was a sighing, sharp and swift, around the ledges, and then silence, in which nothing moved or breathed—only Comyn, running out upon the lip of rock, calling Rogers' name.

Even through the deadening helmet, his voice rang loud and harsh upon the stillness—and the men turned slowly toward it. They had gone very far into whatever strange life they were living now, and they were being called back against their will, and it was a hurt to them. The sheets of fire purled up and over the burning rim, curling above their heads like waves, crested with a bursting foam of light.

111

Their faces were rapt and dreaming, touched now with pain from the hammering of Comyn's voice.

He reached out his gloved hands and set them on Paul's bare shoulders and cried his name again. And the face that looked into his through the leaded glass was the face of Paul Rogers as Comyn had known it all his life, and yet it was not. Paul Rogers was gone from it and someone else was there in his stead, someone beyond his understanding. And Comyn took his hands away and was afraid.

The swift white fires leaped toward the glowing roof, and the people waited on the ledges, and the eyes that had forgotten knowledge and all the ways of men looked into Comyn's and were troubled. Then, as through the opening of a door long closed, recognition came and after it, alarm.

"Not now!" The words were stiff and awkward on Rogers' tongue, but he said them urgently, putting up his hands as though to thrust Comyn back. "No time, not now!"

Vickrey and Kessel—Kessel who had been stout and old beyond his years with study, and who was now lean and timeless and altogether changed—had forgotten Comyn, whose business was not with them. They had turned again to the wonderful bright fire that gave no heat and were looking down into the depths from which it came. The people on the ledges stood unmoving, white shadows painted on the rock, and all their eyes were shining, shining in the light. Comyn cried out. He had not meant to; he had promised Vickrey he would not. But now that Paul was before him in this place the words came whether he would or not.

"Paul, come with me! Come back!"

Paul shook his head. He seemed upset for Comyn's sake, and yet impatient with him too, as though he had committed an unforgivable intrusion.

"Not now, Arch. No time for you to think, no time to talk." His hands pressed hard on Comyn's chest, forcing him back. "I know you. You can't fight them off. Some men, but not you. And you should have time to think first. Go now, hurry!"

Comyn braced his feet. The fire swirl leaped and rushed and quivered all about the jut of rock and in the air above his head. It was hypnotic, beautiful, inviting him as water invites the swimmer. He tried not to look at it. He kept his eyes on Paul, and it was sickening that Paul should be here, wild and naked like the others, his mind and heart both lost in the same quiet madness. It made him angry, and he shouted:

"I've come all the way from Earth to find you. I won't leave you here!"

"Do you want to kill me, Arch?"

That made Comyn stop. He said, "You'd die . . . like Ballantyne? I thought Vickrey said—"

Paul glanced into the abyss and spoke, so rapidly now that Comyn could hardly understand through the helmet audio.

"Not that way. Ballantyne left too soon. I am whole now. But another way, a worse way—Arch, I can't explain now, just go before you're caught, as we were."

"Will you come with me?"

"No."

"Then I'll stay." *Perhaps he's still human enough to remember*, Comyn thought, *perhaps I can make him come that way.*

Paul said, "Look."

He pointed down into the abyss, drawing Comyn closer to the brink. The noiseless white fires whirled and rushed about him, and he stared into them, into a white and blinding glory. And suddenly the world dropped out from under him, and his head reeled with an awful vertigo.

The ledges he had thought were solid rock were only thin curved shells that arched out over a space below, a space that underlay the grotto as the mass of an iceberg underlies its visible small peak, spreading away in a mist of light into secret, unseen reaches. A vault of transuranic fires, burning as though some unknown sun had been caught there, held and treasured by the shielding rock to flame eternally for its own joy, its own wonder, lavishing itself in streams and bursts and torrents of white radiance. Something deep inside of Comyn stirred and woke. He leaned forward and the fear drained out of him, along with many other things that were in his mind. The fire soared and flowed and shifted in the depths of its private world. He could not follow all its motions, but it was beautiful and happy, and good to watch.

And then he yelled and sprang back, and there was no more beauty.

"Something moved!"

"Life," said Paul softly. "Life without need and almost without end. Do you remember the old tale they taught us when we were children—about the people who once lived in a garden of innocence?"

Revulsion was swift and ugly. Comyn shrank back farther from the edge and said, "I'm way beyond that, Paul, and so are you. I think I get it now. This transuranic poisoning —you *are* poisoned, drugged, rotting away inside. You're sinking to the level of these others, and pretty soon there won't be any hope for you. I don't know what the Transuranae do to you, exactly, but the end result is slavery."

He looked up, where the eager ranks were waiting.

"You're worshipping. That's what you're doing. I've seen it before on other worlds, but never quite like this. You're worshipping some stinking nature-force that wrecks your minds while it pleasures your bodies."

He turned, Paul was watching him with a kind of distant pity, his attention already slipping back to the bourne of visions from which Comyn had forced it, and Comyn saw him with disgust, almost with loathing.

"You gave them Strang's body," he said. "And now you're waiting to be paid back."

Paul Rogers sighed. "There is no time at all now, unless you're very swift. Go on, Arch. Run."

Those last commonplace words were inexpressibly shocking. Comyn could remember a thousand times they had been said before, in other places, a measureless time ago. He caught Paul roughly by the arm, this unfamiliar Paul who was lost out of humanity, the Paul of alien flesh and alien worship who could never possibly have been a child with him, and he said:

"You're coming whether you want to or not."

Paul answered quietly, "It's too late."

Strangely, he did not try to fight when Comyn drew him bodily off the jut of rock, away from Vickrey and Kessel.

They came together onto the main ledge and took three steps down the long way to the entrance of the grotto. Then suddenly in that entrance there were men in radiation armor, men with loud voices and heavy boots, coming in along the path—Peter Cochrane and the others from the ship, all armed.

Comyn blundered on, dragging Paul Rogers along the crowded ledge. He only wanted to get out and away from there. He was not sure yet what he was trying to escape from, only that the people were waiting for something and that the thing they waited for was evil and unnatural, and that his whole flesh recoiled from meeting it. The close-ranked bodies stood before him like a wall, between him and the clean outside. He flung himself against that wall and it broke, but it was like a wall of quicksand, flowing tight around him again, holding him fast. He began to sob inside his helmet, caught between the fruitless labor and the fear.

The voices of the men ahead rose up and echoed in the vault. And then there began to be other voices, the voices of the people who had no longer any need of speech to express the simplicity of their emotions. They surged forward a little on the ledges and cried out joyously, and the human sounds were drowned and washed away.

Comyn struggled to break through, but it was too late. It had been too late from the beginning, and he was caught now, caught as Paul had been. He let go of Paul's unresisting arm and turned toward the chasm, bracing himself by sheer instinct to fight whatever came up out of it. And then, for a moment, he forgot even to be afraid.

For suddenly, the place was filled with stars.

There had been light before, enough to blind a man, but not like this. There had been motion before, in the rushing fires, but not like this. The eager pressing of the people bore him on almost to the edge, but he was beyond caring. The breath and the wits together were gone out of him, and he could only stare and wonder like a child.

In a cloud they came, whirling upward through the white aurora. And they were whiter; they were pure with primal radiance, and their raying arms were like the misty nebulae.

Soaring they came, carried up on the waves of fire, and they paled it. Laughing they came, and their laughter was the laughter of young things fresh and new from the hand of God, not knowing any darkness.

These were strange thoughts for Comyn to be thinking, who had left all such imaginings behind with the first sprouting of his beard. But for some reason he thought them now. The laughter was soundless, but it was there. It was in the way they moved and shone and gave forth light.

White stars bursting through a sky of flame, and one last pealing cry of welcome from the ledges. And Paul Rogers spoke and said:

"These are the Transuranae."

The forces that were in the beginning, the life seed, the fountainhead. Perhaps all men were their children, long removed. Comyn struggled to regain himself, but his head was full of scraps of forgotten things and tatters of old emotions. And he did not know why this should be, except for the shining of the Transuranae and the happy way they danced.

The cloud of stars rushed upward, spread and widened, and their misty arms reached out to touch and twine. They wheeled about each other, spun and parted and rejoined, not with any reason or design except that they lived and it was pleasure. And the brightness was such that Comyn bowed beneath it, drugged also with a strange new pleasure.

Peter Cochrane moved slowly in toward the chasm, and with him came the other men in armor. Their eyes were on the Transuranae. Vaguely Comyn saw them, and he knew that they could not go away now, even though the path was clear. He knew that he could not have gone himself.

Paul's hand was on him and his voice was in his ears. "You'll understand now. In a minute you will understand."

There was another surging forward of the people, a final motion that bore Comyn to the extreme edge. And now, upon the farther ledge, beyond the chasm, he saw an armored shape revealed by the shifting of the crowd. It was pressed back against the rock wall, and Comyn knew who it must be: Stanley, who had come there before all of them to find the place of the Transuranae; Stanley, who had found it, and whose rifle now trailed forgotten from his hands.

Paul's hand tightened briefly on Comyn's arm. Comyn looked at him. Paul was smiling and in his face was something of the shining of the Transuranae. He said, "I'm sorry you had no chance to decide. But Arch, I'm glad you came." That was the last he said. There was no more time for speech. Comyn looked up, dizzy with the wheeling of great stars. And then the stars fell, out of the burning vault.

Down they plunged in a rain of living fire, a galaxy dropping down the sky, rushing, leaping as meteors leap in curving flight, crashing down in glory upon the place below: on Comyn, stunned beneath that flaming fall; on the people standing naked, with their arms uplifted to receive delight.

And the Transuranae spread wide their own arms that were like the arms of nebulae and wrapped them round, and the people faded and were indistinct, lost each one in the heart of a star. Comyn was among them, cloaked in apocalyptic fire.

He stood transfixed for as long as his heart might beat three times. In him was something crying to break free, to welcome the magnificence that had so suddenly blotted out the world. And then the strong coarse part of Comyn that had been dazed a little while shook off its dreaming, and he voiced a strangled cry of horror. He struck out at the thing that held him, wrenching away in a perfect madness of revulsion.

He did not want to be like Ballantyne. He did not want to be like Paul, with the soul and the mind sapped out of him. He did not want to be Strang, cast still moving into the abyss to be an offering to stars.

He clawed and tore at the supernal brilliance that covered him. And it was brilliance and nothing more, and his hands passed through it as through smoke. He tried again to run, and the closed-packed bodies barred him in, locked him in some awful union with the Transuranae. There was no way out.

He screamed to Paul for help, but Paul was gone behind a veil of light, and there was no help.

Trapped, beyond hope, Comyn waited. His armor was heavy, and it was strong, but these were transuranic forces that no one understood and their radiations were unknown. Already, faint and filtered through the ray-proof fabric, he could sense a power . . .

It grew. Comyn steeled himself, staring through the leaded helmet plate into a blinding nexus of beauty such as he had never dreamed, and the tremendous energies that poured out from that beauty began to touch and stir him.

It was a warming touch, like the first bright sun breaking through the chill of winter. He could feel it stealing through his body, into the fear-taut places of his mind, and where it went there was no more room for tension or for fear. The fire that held him in its misty arms flooded him with a white radiance, and gradually a very strange truth was revealed to Comyn. There was no evil in the Transuranae.

The tide of warmth, of life, surged through him—only the faint far edges of it, dammed back by the armor, but enough. The white glory beat upon him through the helmet plate, and he began to understand. He knew why Paul could never go back. He knew why the eyes of the people disturbed him, why Vickrey's eyes had been so strange. He knew why these people no longer needed the ways of cities and of men. The forces that were in the beginning, the life seed, the fountainhead . . .

His body lifted and strained toward the light. His flesh desired the fiery clean brilliance that was there, the power that changed, that entered into every cell and drove out hunger and sickness and all need, and put life in its place. He wanted the full force of that power to surge through him, as it surged through the bodies of the people. He wanted to be free as Paul was free.

The forests are there and the plains, a world open and unfettered, unstained by blood or tortured by many harvests. No more hunger, no more lust, no more hard necessity. Only the sun by day and the copper moons by night, and time without end, without sorrow, and only the faintest shadow of a forgotten thing called death.

Some hard resistant core of mind that could still remember through all the vision of a new existence gave back his own words to him: *You're way beyond that. Innocence was too long ago and too well lost. This isn't a man's life. It may be better, but it isn't for man. It's alien. Don't touch it.*

But Comyn understood now that what he had called degeneracy was something far different, that what he had called worship was the welcoming of friends, that what he had thought of as an offering was only a giving back of life to the scouring fires whence it came. The world of the Transuranae was beckoning to him, and he would not listen to that one dissenting voice.

The star blaze that entered through his helmet plate was burning now within his brain, and all doubt was drowned in whiteness. He knew that he was not being tempted, but that he was being offered a gift unknown since Eden. He lifted his hands and laid them on the fastenings of his armor.

Someone caught his hands. Someone shouted, and he was dragged away, out of the misty arms that wrapped him, and the star blaze dimmed. He struggled, crying out, and Peter Cochrane's face came close to his. He saw it distorted and wild behind the helmet glass. Peter Cochrane's voice screamed at him. Wheeling stars were lifting all about him, and on either side the people gave back, some still folded in the bright arms. Behind him others lay stunned on the ledge, and there were armored men with rifles.

He fought to tear his armor off. In their blindness they were afraid. Cochrane was afraid, as Ballantyne had been afraid. They feared, and they wanted to force him back to humanity and death.

"Comyn! Don't you know what you're doing? Look there!"

He looked across the chasm. Stanley was no longer pressed against the rock. He stood with the people and he had taken off his armor.

"He's lost! Others too before we realized." Sweat ran down on Peter's face, and it was gray with some inner anguish. He was dragging at Comyn, trying to force him back, talking disjointedly about saving him. He had saved others with the rifles.

Across the abyss, Stanley raised his arms to a soaring star. It rushed down and Stanley was like the others, a white form half hidden in living fire.

"Lost—"

"Look at his face!" cried Comyn. "He's not lost, but you are. You are! Let me go!"

"Crazy. I know. I can feel it myself." Peter thrust him farther back, desperately, as one would thrust another from the pit. "Don't fight me, Comyn. The others are beyond help, but—" He struck hard with his hand on Comyn's helmet. "It isn't life they offer. It's negation, a pointless wandering—"

Comyn looked up at the Transuranae. There was a time before, in the far beginning, a time before labor and pain and fear . . .

They did not understand because they had too much fear in them. But he could not stay for them. He flung himself away from the restraining hands. He went out toward the chasm, wrenching at the stubborn closures of his armor. Behind him a rifle rose and flashed.

The armor was proof against radiation, but not proof at all against the different violence of the shock-guns. The fires of the grotto faded, and Comyn went out into the darkness, agonizing for the stars that he had touched and lost forever.

XV

COMYN AWOKE to pain. It was not only the sharp stinging of his whole body but also the persistent gnawing in his ears and brain of a sound that was not quite sound.

He knew what it was. He didn't want to know. He wanted to deny it and make it not, but he knew. The sound of the star-drive. The star-drive, the ship . . .

He had to open his eyes. He didn't want to do that either, but he did. The metal ceiling of his cabin was above him, and against it was French's face looking down.

"Well, Comyn."

He was trying to be commonplace, casual, but he wasn't a good actor and there was something in his expression.

"Well, Comyn, I think you're clean. Roth and I have had to work. But luckily for you, you only got a touch of it, and I think we've sweated and purged the last poison out of you . . ."

Comyn said, "Get the hell out of here."

"Now listen! You've had a shock, and it stands to reason—"

"Get out."

French's face went away, and there was a murmuring of voices and a door closing . . . and then nothing but the insidious, inaudible screech of the drive.

Comyn lay still and tried not to think about it, not to remember. But he had to remember. He couldn't forget that rain of stars out of a sky of flame, that clean ecstasy, the shining around him and the joy . . .

He was nuts. He was lucky to get away; he might have become like Ballantyne. He told himself that. But he couldn't help thinking of Paul, of the others on that world that was falling farther back with every second. Paul and the others were freed, living in a way nobody else could ever live, under a sky of copper moons.

He wanted to break down, to sob like a dame, but he couldn't. He wanted to sleep, but he couldn't do that either. After a time, Peter Cochrane came. Peter was not one to gentle people. He came and stood, looking down with no kindness in his dark, Indian face, and said:

"So you feel bad. You feel bad because you're Arch Comyn, a very tough guy, and you fell apart like a kid when you really came up against it."

Comyn looked at him and didn't say anything. He didn't have to, it seemed. There must have been something in his eyes. For Peter's face changed.

"Look, Comyn, I can make you feel better about that. French says that the ones of us who fell apart were the ones who didn't have *enough* fear—not enough caution, enough inhibitions, to keep us scared of it."

Comyn asked, "Stanley?"

Peter said, "Yes. We left him there." And then his voice got raw-edged. "What else could we do? He'd had it, full force, and if we took him he'd be Ballantyne all over again. Better to let him stay, as he wanted. As it was, we barely got you away in time."

Comyn said, "And you came in here now to get thanked for saving me?" Peter's face grew angry, but Comyn went on, all his blind passion gathering. "You reached inside the gates and snatched a man out of a kind of life no man ever dreamed before of having, and you want him to thank you?"

He was sitting up now, and he rushed on before Peter could interrupt. "You know what? You were scared, too scared to quit being a mucky little person named Peter Cochrane, too scared to walk out of the grubby little life you knew. And because you were, you dream it up now that it was poison, it was evil, it mustn't be touched, no one must touch it."

Peter did not answer. He stood looking down at Comyn. and then his face grew haunted, haggard, and his shoulders sagged a little.

"I think," he whispered after a moment, "I think you may be right. But, Comyn . . ."

Peter had been fighting his own battle. Comyn saw that now. His dark face was gaunt from strain and something more than strain.

". . . but Comyn, should a man be more—or less—than a man? Even if the Transuranae were the shining good they seemed, even if they could make men like angels, it seems wrong, wrong, for men to step so suddenly out of what the cosmos has made them. Maybe, ages from now, we could be like that. But now, it seems wrong."

"In Adam's fall, we sinned all," quoted Comyn harshly. "Sure. Stick to it. It's the only life we know, so it's the best one. The people of Barnard II won't build any star-ships or any castles on the moon. So that makes us better. Or does it?"

Peter nodded heavily. "It's a question. But when I had to answer it, there was only one way I could decide. I think in time you'll agree." He paused and added, "Ballantyne did. Either his armor failed, or he took it off, because he'd had the first full dose. But he couldn't stay inside the gates of paradise. Maybe it wasn't so good when he took another look at it."

"Maybe," said Comyn, without conviction. He remembered Stanley's face at the last minute: a wretched little man with a lot of hounding passions he couldn't satisfy, inadequate and eaten up with envy, and yet there at the end he had found something better than a share in Cochrane Transuranic or anything else he had wanted. He had simply stopped being Stanley. And now he was there and Comyn was here, and Comyn hated Stanley in a curious new way.

Peter turned. "French says you're all right to move around. Don't stay in here and sulk. It only makes it worse."

Comyn cursed him with all his heart, and Peter smiled faintly. "I don't think you'd have made a really satisfactory angel," he said, and left.

Comyn sat on the bunk and put his face between his hands, and in the darkness behind his eyes he saw again the swift white fires leaping and the fierce and splendid burning of the stars. Something shook him like a great hand and left him empty.

He didn't want to move around. He didn't want to go back to doing the things he'd done before, and he didn't want to see anybody. But he did want a drink. He wanted a drink very badly, and there wasn't any where he was, so he got up and went outside.

Whatever French and Roth had done to him had left

him weak as a baby. Everything seemed dim around him, touched with unreality. In the main cabin, he found a bunch of the others sitting around, looking like men who had been sick. They looked at him and then looked away again, as though he reminded them of something they didn't want to remember.

There was a bottle on the table. It had already been punished hard. Comyn put down most of what was left in it. It didn't make him feel any better, but it numbed him so he didn't care how he felt. He glanced around, but nobody looked at him or said anything to him.

Comyn said, "Knock it off, will you. I won't explode."

There were a couple of feeble grins and a pretense of greeting, and then they went back to their thinking again. Comyn began to realize that they weren't thinking about him as much as they were about themselves.

One of them spoke up. "I want to know—I want to know what we saw. Those things . . ."

French sighed. "We all want to know. And we never will, not completely. But . . ." He paused, then said, "They weren't things. They were life, a form of life inconceivable except among the alien elements of a transuranic world. Life, I think, seated in linkages of energy between atoms infinitely more complex than uranium. Life, self-sufficient, perhaps coeval with our universe, and able to impregnate our cruder, simpler tissues with its own transuranic chemistry . . ."

Comyn thought again of what Vickrey had said: the fountainhead, the beginning.

Someone said grimly, "I know one thing: no one's getting me back there, for anything."

Peter Cochrane said, "Relax. Nobody's going back to Barnard II."

But, when Comyn was again alone with Peter, he said, "You're wrong. In the end, I'll go back."

Peter shook his head. "You think you will. You're still under its touch. But that will fade."

"No."

But it did. It faded; as the timeless hours went by, it faded . . . as he ate and slept and went through all the motions of being human. Not the memory of it; that did not dim. But the fierce, aching pull of a life beyond life couldn't hold a man every minute, not when he was shaving, not when he was taking off his shoes, not when he was drunk.

There came an end at last to the timelessness and the waiting. They suffered again through the eerie wrenchings and vertiginous shifts and came out of drive into normal space. And presently Luna shone like a silver shield beyond the forward ports, and the second Big Jump was finished.

After the long confinement of the ship the eruption of new voices and unfamiliar faces was confusing. The gardens hadn't changed in the million years Comyn had been away, nor the bulk of the great house in the blaze of the lunar day. Comyn walked through it all like a stranger, and yet everything was the same except himself.

He was not the only one who felt that way. It was a joyless business. They had brought back with them from a foreign sun the same chill shadow that had covered Ballantyne, and Claudia was wailing loud over the death of Stanley. They had told her he was dead, and in a sense it was quite true. They had not conquered any stars. A star had conquered them.

Comyn searched among the faces for one he did not see, and somebody told him, "She wouldn't stay here after the ship took off. She said the place was haunted, and that she couldn't stand it. She went back to New York."

Comyn said, "I know exactly what she meant."

The halls of the great house were cool and dim, and Comyn would have waited in them alone, but Peter said:

"I may need you, Comyn. You were closer to it than any of us, and Jonas won't be easy to convince."

Reluctantly, Comyn stood once more in the crowded, old-fashioned room that looked out over the Mare Imbrium, and Jonas was as he had been before: an ancient dusty man huddled in a chair, more frail, more wrinkled, slipping farther over that ultimate dark edge. But still he raked with his claw-like hands at life, still he burned with ambition.

"You got it, eh?" he said to Peter, leaning his cage of

bones forward in the chair. "Cochrane Transuranic! Has a good sound, doesn't it? How much, Peter? Tell me how much!"

Peter said slowly, "We didn't get it, Grandfather. The world is . . . poisoned. Ballantyne's crew and three of our own men—" He paused, and then muttered the fictional word. "There won't be any Cochrane Transuranic, now or ever."

For a long moment Jonas was utterly still, and the color surged up into his face until it threatened to burst the parchment skin. Comyn felt a distant pang of pity for him. He was such an old man, and he wanted so much to steal a star before he died.

"You let it go," said Jonas, and he cursed Peter with all the breath he had. Coward was the kindest word. "All right, I'll find a man who's not afraid. I'll send out another ship—"

"No," said Peter. "I'm going down to talk to the Government men. There'll be other voyages to other stars, but Barnard's must be let alone. The radioactive contamination there is a kind nobody can fight."

Jonas' withered lips still moved, but no sound came out of them, and his body jerked in a perfect paroxysm of rage. Peter said wearily:

"I'm sorry, but it's so."

"Sorry," whispered Jonas. "If I were young again, if I could only stand, I'd find a way . . ."

"You wouldn't," said Comyn sharply. Suddenly a passion came over him. He remembered many things and he bent over Jonas fiercely and said, "There are some things even the Cochranes aren't big enough to handle. You wouldn't understand if I explained to you, but that world is safe for all time, from everybody. And Peter's right."

He turned and left the room, and Peter came after him. Comyn made a gesture of distaste, and said, "Let's go."

When they landed in New York, when they finally got clear of the mob scene that went on for a time around the spaceport, Comyn told Peter:

"You go on to your Government men. I got better things to do."

"But if they want you too—"

"I'll be in the Rocket Room's bar."

Later, sitting in the bar, Comyn kept his back to the video, but he couldn't shut out the breathless voice that tumbled out the news to all the gaping, excited listeners.

". . . *and this magnificent second voyage, while it explored only a radioactive-poisoned world that cannot be exploited or visited again, is still another great trail blazed to the stars. Other ships will soon be going out there, other men . . .*"

Comyn thought that sure, they'd go, all full of neat little schemes. But they'd find out that it wasn't the same as their little planets. They'd find they were out in the big league and that human games were not played out there.

He didn't turn, not right away, when a throaty voice at his shoulder interrupted.

"Buy me a drink, Comyn?"

When he did turn he saw it was Sydna. She looked just the same. She wore a white dress that revealed her brown shoulders, and her improbable hair was the color of flax, and she had that cool, lazy smile.

"I'll buy you a drink," he said. "Sure. Sit down."

She did and lit a cigarette, and then looked at him through the drifting smoke.

"You don't look quite so good, Comyn."

"Don't I?"

"Peter said that you found something pretty bad out there."

"Yeah. So bad that we didn't dare to stay, so bad we had to run right back to Earth."

"But you found Paul Rogers?"

"I found him."

"But you didn't bring him back?"

"No."

She picked up her drink. "All right. Tactful Sydna, who knows when to keep her mouth shut. Here's to you."

After a moment, she said, "I found out something too, Comyn. You're a rather ugly roughneck—"

"I thought you knew that."

"I did. But what I found out was that in spite of it, I missed you."

"So?"

"Oh, hell, I can't keep being coy," she said. "I'm leading up to the idea of getting married. I've thought about it. It'd be so much more convenient."

"Have you got enough money that I wouldn't have to work?" he asked.

"Plenty, Comyn."

"Well, that's something," he said. "Though I'd probably get tired of spending it and go back to work anyway. There's only one thing . . ."

"Yes?"

"You ought to know something, Sydna. I'm not the same guy you got acquainted with. I got rearranged a little inside."

"It doesn't show much."

"It will. You didn't like it up in your lunar castle because it was haunted. How will you like living with a haunted man?"

"I'll unhaunt you, Comyn."

"Can you?"

"It'll be fun trying. Let's have another."

He turned and signaled the waiter and turned back to her, and the strange pain took him by the throat again: the pain of loss, of exile, of a fading longing.

I'm slipping back, back all the way to Arch Comyn, and I don't want to! I'm forgetting what it was like, what it could have been like, and all my life I'll think of it and want to go back, and be afraid to . . .

Let it go, he thought, let it go and slip back. It might be second-rate to be just human but it's comfortable, it's comfortable . . .

He looked across the table at Sydna. "Shall we drink on it?"

She nodded and reached out her free hand. And when he took it, it quivered inside his grasp. She said:

"All of a sudden, I don't want another drink. I want to cry."

She did.